One Summer

BAKER GIRL SERIES, BOOK 1

MARY JANE FORBES

Todd Book Publications

ONE SUMMER

ISBN: 978-0692284872 (sc)
Printed in the United States of America
Todd Book Publications: 9/2014
Port Orange, Florida

Author photo: Geri Rogers
© Cleaper | Dreamstime.com
Retro Vintage American Diner And Jukebox Photo
© llaszlo background
© Paha_L counter stools

Dedication

To: The Diner Sleuths

Marcia Campbell
Peggy Keeney
Jeanne O'Brien

A springtime visit turned into a challenge
to come up with a storyline for my new novel.

Over coffee the ideas flew about.
Over lunch the story came to life.
Then, in a diner,
over a decadent piece of chocolate fudge cake,
with whipped cream and a cherry on top, emerged

One Summer

Books by Mary Jane Forbes

DroneKing Trilogy
A Toy for Christmas, A Ghostly Affair
Love is in the Air

Bradley *Farm Series*
Bradley Farm, Sadie, Finn
Jeli, Marshall, Georgie

Baker Girl Series
One Summer
Promises

Twists of Fate Series
The Fisherman, a love story
The Witness, living a lie
Twists of Fate

Murder by Design, Series:
Murder by Design
Labeled in Seattle
Choices, And the Courage to Risk

Novels
The Mailbox
Black Magic, An Arabian Stallion
The Painter
The Baby Quilt ... a mystery!
The Message...Call Me!
Twister

House of Beads Mystery Series
Murder in the House of Beads
Intercept, Checkmate, Identity Theft

Short Stories
Once Upon a Christmas Eve, a Romantic Fairy Tale
The Christmas Angel and the Magic Holiday Tree
RJ, The Little Hero

Visit: www.MaryJaneForbes.com

One Summer

Chapter 1

FIRED!

Star's spanky-new white sneakers slapped the sidewalk, her arms tight around a dinged-up black duffle bag.

"Hey, Blondie, want a ride?" The red love-wagon slowed alongside her, three young punks hanging out the windows. Another man-boy called out the driver's window, "Come on-Blondie. Wherever you're going, we're going."

Without a glance, Star flipped a bird at the jerks and was immediately horrified at her slutty salvo. *Gran would die if she saw what I just did. Get a grip, Star.*

Ten minutes ago, she had held her head high, marched out of the hotel kitchen, marched through the dining room, marched out the marbled lobby into the bright sunshine.

Fired!

She'd show them someday.

She'd serve a fancy French pastry to a queen, well, maybe not a queen but definitely someone rich and famous.

Sexual harassment!

Fired for harassing pimply-faced Howard Boggs. Over the past month, he had ratted on her numerous times for changing the ingredients—a pinch of this or that, adding bits of flavor. He had the imagination of a toad. Howie—all he wanted was to get her between the sheets. He didn't get what the word NO meant. Kept pinching her butt. And the nerve—pushing her into the racks of flour and sugar, trying to feel her up, trying to kiss her. But she showed him. Oh yeah, he felt that knee in his crotch.

Sexual harassment?

She should have ratted on him, then he would have been the one to get fired. Or, maybe not. The pimple-faced toad was the nephew of the head chef.

Now, I'm out of a job. Not a job. My dream job. Out on the street making ugly gestures.

The grind of car engines, the smell of exhaust, signaled traffic building on Atlantic Avenue. The street crowded with bikini-clad girls laughing, strolling in groups down the alleys to the beach. Following very close behind the bikinis were Tarzan-like boys, joking, making sly remarks carrying surfboards under their arms or over their heads. Spring break would end soon followed by young graduates celebrating their freedom, their escape from ivy-covered buildings.

Arriving next, families carting kids, lots of kids. After all, Disney World was only an hour away.

Tourists flocking to the east coast of Florida, flocking to the land of sunshine.

Paradise!

The streets, sidewalks, sand, and surf beckoning, welcoming the visitors.

What am I going to do? What am I going to do? What am I going to do?

Last day of April. Restaurants were staffed for tourist season, managers training young servers proper etiquette—etiquette guaranteed to keep the customer ordering more, etiquette so the customer rewarded the server with an extra tip, a tip that still had to be divided between the kitchen staff. Spring-breakers arrived every week for fun in the sun, strolling to the Daytona Beach boardwalk, buying trinkets, riding the Ferris wheel, swaying to concerts at the Bandshell. Merchants were ready to rake in the dough from the breakers, from the tourists with kids, all with money in their pockets, eager to spend.

Money. Star had exactly three dollars and forty-five cents in her duffel coin pouch, maybe a hundred-twenty-six in her checking account. Her savings account was almost depleted with the purchase of a top-of-the-line mixer she just had to have in her studio's tiny kitchen corner, had to have to experiment baking pastries, breads, cakes, cookies with special flavorings.

Fighting back tears, fighting the panic gripping her chest, Star tried unsuccessfully to breathe deep. Gulps of air only increased the nausea growing in her belly. One thing was for sure, she was not going back to Hoboken to face him. "I told you not to go to Florida. Be a pastry chef? You need a real job," her father had grumbled for the umpteenth time. Her mother didn't care one way or the other. Only her Gran understood her desire to be a baker, a baker like she had always dreamed of being when she was Star's age.

"Oh, God, what am I going to do?" Star muttered.

"Hey, Sugar, want a ride?" With no reply from Sugar, the yellow Chevy accelerated, leaving the blonde, her hair pulled back with a black bow, her white shirt sticking to her back with sweat, head down, walking mindlessly in the opposite direction.

Rent was due today. The empty refrigerator was waiting to be fed.

Shop windows passed in and out of view with their displays of brightly colored T-shirts—Daytona Beach printed in a rainbow of colors curving over a bright yellow sun—ready to lure in and snare the breakers' loose cash.

Star passed a small sign scribbled in the corner of a souvenir shop window: *Help wanted*.

Her arms tightened again around the duffle bag. "No. No. No shop girl. I'm a pastry chef for heaven's sake!"

Her feet carried her forward. Crossed the street, passed a blow-up clown triggering his electronic voice, "Hi, come on in."

Crossed another street.

Passed a silver diner.

Stopping abruptly, Star turned, stared at the sign in the diner's window: *Wanted, Waitress*.

Why not? She had a stellar record at the Manatee Bar and Grill a couple miles south. She had been their top cocktail waitress. They would give her a good recommendation. She didn't have to mention the hotel restaurant ... unless they asked. A quick waitress job would pay the rent, buy frozen pizzas for the fridge. Her little rental was only three blocks away.

Why not?

A man in a wheelchair, the wheels at cross purposes to the diner's door, was struggling to reach the handle. His biceps straining against the plaid short-sleeved shirt attested to his workouts pushing the wheel of his chair. Marching up the handicap-accessible cement ramp, Star grasped the chair's worn leather handlebars at the same time someone inside opened the door to leave. Catching the door with her hip, Star pushed the man through onto the black and white squares of tile.

"Hi, Benny. The usual?" A lanky waiter called over his shoulder scooting by with two plates of sandwiches, French fries on the side.

"You bet." Benny grinned up at his helper. His thick salt and pepper hair grazed his shoulders touching tufts of gray hair on his chin.

"And where do you usually sit for your usual?" Star asked returning the grin, her blue eyes crinkling.

"That little table, miss. End of the counter. It's my spot, but I can—"

Stepping across the black and white tiles, chin lifted, Star pushed the man to his spot, and then sat on the vinyl cow-hide patterned stool at the end of the counter. Shoving her duffle down on the floor between her feet, she glanced around. Two o'clock, the place was practically deserted—after lunch, before dinner she surmised.

"Thanks, miss," Benny said, leaning toward the counter. I usually don't have a problem. Dang chair just wouldn't follow my orders today."

"My pleasure, sir." She smiled glancing at his suspenders pulling his plaid shirt across his chest accentuating the muscles she saw when he was struggling with his chair. His muscular arms a sharp contrast to the skinny legs that dropped to the foot supports. No matter the wheelchair, Benny had a sweet smile that included a twinkle in his pale gray eyes.

The lanky young waiter, bony elbows sticking out from his white short-sleeved shirt, a black bow tie a bit askew, served Benny a mug of coffee then hustled behind the counter to his blonde customer. *Tyler* was printed in black on his white name tag clipped to the pocket of his shirt. "What can I get for you, miss?" he asked with a broad smile peering at her through thick horn-rimmed glasses. A shock of dark-brown hair tickled his right eyebrow.

"Coffee, please. I noticed the sign ... about a waitress. Is the manager in?"

"Sure is. I'll tell him and get you that coffee. Would that be with cream and sugar? Sugar packets right here and those little creamers are fresh. I personally refreshed the dish a few minutes ago. Unless you'd like a flavored creamer—"

"Black is good. Thanks." Star smiled inside. The waiter looked to be around her age—mid to late twenties—trying very hard to make a good impression, perhaps worried he was going to be let go, what with the wanted sign in the window for a waitress.

Tyler hustled to the coffee station at the other end of the counter, stopping only long enough to pass the young woman's request to a man scrubbing down the grill behind the order window. "Charlie, girl at the counter wants to be a waitress."

Star rolled her eyes. She didn't *want* to be a waitress, she *needed* to be a waitress, at least for a week or two while she looked for a new pastry chef position.

Charlie looked over at Star, squinted, threw down the scouring pad and wiped his hands on the towel hooked under the belt of his white bib apron. Eggs were definitely on the menu earlier along with hot dogs and mustard. The man called Charlie sauntered over to her. "Hi. Looking for a job?"

"Yes, sir. I'm back in town, and my regular job at the Manatee was filled."

"Ah, experienced. When are you looking to start, because I need someone right—"

"Right away, sir. You can call the Manatee for a reference. Do you know the manager, Mr.—"

"Sure do. Hold on a sec while I get Wanda. She hires the staff, except for the cooks. I interview all the short-order guys. What's your name, miss?"

"Star Bloom."

Charlie smiled. He thought he'd heard all the fancy names, but this was a new one. He shuffled away disappearing behind the grill window.

Star opened a little creamer cup. Why not—just this once? On her feet all day hustling in the restaurant's kitchen she didn't have to watch her weight. She was mindful, but seemed able to maintain a slim figure without a problem. Adding the cream to her coffee, her eyes roved over the red, blue, and purple neon tubing around the tin ceiling, at the red vinyl booths, several little white Formica bistro tables with red vinyl chairs tucked neatly in place. The diner was clean, inviting, charming really.

She and Benny exchanged glances. He gave her a nod of encouragement.

A woman, shuffling along same as Charlie, emerged from the back wiping her hands on a red and white striped dish towel. Star guessed her to be the same age as Charlie, late forties ... hard to tell. Both appeared tired, circles under their eyes.

"Hi, Star Bloom is it?"

"Yes. I saw the sign in the window and—"

"Honey, my name's Wanda, and I already called the Manatee. The bartender couldn't say enough nice things about you. If you have a minute, let's sit over at that first booth. Ty, can you bring me a cup of coffee, please? Thanks."

Star warmed immediately to the woman. She was respectful to Tyler, saying please, respect she sorely wanted, given the day she'd had. Plus Wanda was quick to act when she saw a potential waitress, already calling for a reference.

"We run with a pretty small crew—Charlie and I step in if we're shorthanded. We have a part-time cook, Harry. He's a retired school teacher, likes a few hours now and then. He takes a shift on weekends, fills in some. Charlie generally cooks the second shift on those days ... when Harry's on the grill. We have three waitresses—Kim, Brenda, and Claire ... not quite full time. When it's slow, they have fewer hours, or vice versa. If we're busy, they get more."

"Wanda, I'm looking for full time. In fact, I'm looking for as many hours as I can get."

"Honey, that's music to my ears."

"I can fill in on short notice, come in early, stay late—whatever it takes. I need the money."

"In a pinch, we have a few high school seniors we can call, that is they'll be seniors when they go back to school. But, it would be nice to have someone, once you learn the ropes, to help keep the operation running without too many hiccups. If you know what I mean?"

"Oh, I know, I know. It was murder at the Manatee when a waitress didn't show up, especially at the bar."

• • •

EVERYTHING HAPPENED FAST. Wanda said two of their waitresses had left without notice. In spite of the spring-breakers, business had slowed, and she knew the tips would not be what Star was used to receiving at the bar. Downright meager in comparison were her words. Tyler couldn't work twelve-hour shifts, seven days a week. She and Charlie, a husband and wife team, needed immediate help.

With an experienced waitress sitting across from her, and armed with praise from another establishment, Wanda was eager to hire the girl before someone else snatched her up. "Nothing fancy here. None of those colorful umbrella concoctions you served at the Manatee. As a trial, could you do a dinner shift from five to nine tonight? Get your feet wet? With pay, of course. If I like what I see, and if you like what you see, we'll talk tomorrow. But, I have one stipulation."

"Sounds fine so far. Yes, I can work tonight. What is the stipulation?"

"You have to agree to stay four months, through the height of tourist season. We have enough to worry about without a revolving door, hiring, training, leaving. I'm sure you can understand."

Star's eyes slid up to the ceiling, at the red, to blue, to purple neon pulsating through the glass tubes. Small, white ceiling fans gently swirled the air picking up a mixture of scents from the grill—bacon, French fries, and an occasional slice of meatloaf. It certainly wasn't a five-star hotel restaurant, and she was sure another pastry-chef position was not going to come calling this close to the height of the season. Meager tips Wanda said. But, it would give her a chance to find something better in the fall when the big turnover of restaurant staff occurred. And, who knows, maybe she'd decide to return to Hoboken, go back to her family. *Not!*

"Star, what do you say? Interested? Ty could show you around."

"Yes, Wanda. I'll be back at five. And, we'll talk tomorrow."

"Good. I'll tell Tyler. He'll top off that coffee—on the house." As Wanda shuffled away, she stopped briefly, whispered something to her husband flipping a burger on the grill, and then disappeared down a short hall.

Star caught Benny grinning at her again and joined him at the little retro bistro table.

"Sounds to me like a celebration is in order, Star Bloom. Here, put this quarter in the jukebox, the old Wurlitzer by the front door. Punch B39." Fishing the coin out of his pants pocket, Benny placed the twenty-five cent piece in Star's open palm.

Johnny Cash drawled out, “A Boy Named Sue” as the two chatted and giggled. Star rose, gave Benny a kiss on the cheek, grabbed her duffle, waved at Charlie and left, overhearing Benny say something like he’d never wash that cheek again.

Chapter 2

THREE DAYS, THREE SHIFTS.

Ambling along Atlantic Avenue from her studio apartment, Star felt herself relaxing, pushing the charge of sexual harassment behind her. Her new job was fun. Who would have thought interaction with the customers could be enjoyable.

She had always visualized herself behind the scenes, in the kitchen surrounded by gleaming copper pots, the flicker of controlled flames from the gas burners gently melting chocolate squares for her latest dessert, scents of vanilla and ginger along with the aroma of garlic and onion from the other chef's entrées. She had never witnessed the patrons experiencing the food, closing their eyes, savoring the flavor melting on their tongue.

The diner was also planets away from serving at the Manatee Bar. The guests at the diner were friendly, engaging her in lively conversation—where to find the best hot dog, here of course. T-shirts—next door. Trinkets—two shops down. Now and then a couple argued across French toast, but leaving hand in hand after their last sip of coffee.

No butt pinchers. Husbands and wives, enjoying each other's company, planned their day, as opposed to men out to make a score following a few drinks. At least as far as she could tell, that's how it was at the diner.

The first day had morphed into two, then three. She bonded quickly with Charlie and Wanda. Turned out they were the owners of the silver diner. They genuinely seemed to like her too.

Now a new day, a spring in her step, a smile bubbling with thoughts of her new job, she approached the diner's glass door rimmed with shiny stainless steel. She grinned at her reflection. *Not bad. A slim blonde Florida girl, nice tan in spite of the hours spent in a kitchen.*

Sunday morning, a 7:00 a.m. opening on a bright, sunny May day. The cool salty ocean breeze wafting over Daytona Beach held the humidity at bay, for a few hours anyway.

Tyler was easygoing. Wanda scheduled the two waiters to overlap the lunch shift. Behind his intense look through his black-rimmed glasses, Ty was a man who seemed to find humor in most everything as long as the *i* was dotted and the *t* crossed. Precise with everything in his life, he dressed neatly as a proud penguin—white short-sleeved shirt, always a black bow tie a little askew, a pair of black slacks with a sharp crease down the leg.

The morning crowd filtered into the diner—their chatter punctuated with laughter, always holding out their mugs for refills when Star made the rounds offering a fresh brew of coffee. Still learning the ropes, few as they were, she didn't mind that the crowd was shrinking, gave her more time to cater to her guests.

Star had noticed the day she first helped Benny through the door that there were many empty seats. She thought the diner delightful and couldn't figure out why there wasn't standing room only. Maybe it was Jonny, the early morning cook. Orders were filled quickly when Charlie was behind the grill. But tension seemed to float heavy in the air when Jonny flipped the burgers.

The regulars soon called Star by name, asking for another pat of butter, or more strawberry jam for their toast and muffins. *A real hometown feeling*, Star thought.

A little after nine o'clock, an olive-skinned man entered, his eyes darting around the diner. An older man sitting at the counter, stood, reached into his pants pocket, dropped a few coins by his empty plate. Picking up his bill he walked to the cash register a few feet away. "Thanks, Star. Have a good day." Smiling, he passed the newcomer who slid onto the vacated stool.

Star picked up the change, empty mug, and plate, and flashed a smile at the new customer. "Coffee?"

"Yes, thanks."

She glanced at him as she poured steaming coffee into a mug. "Haven't seen you before. Vacationing?"

"Not really, Finished school, threw a dart at a map, and here I am."

"Come on. A dart?"

"Not really. Looking for a job. Any tips?"

"First tip, put the diner down as your go-to-place."

"Go to?"

"Sure, the place to go to when you're hungry while looking for a job. What's your name?"

"Ash."

"Okay, Ash. What kind of work are you looking for?"

"Anything at the moment."

"What would you like for breakfast this morning? Our special breakfast plate—"

"Coffee is all for now, thanks."

He looks hungry. Just coffee? Low on money" I know how that feels. School he said—looks a little old for school. He has at least a year on me, maybe thirty. Nice smile though, Star thought. "Okay. Refills are on the house."

Star leaned against the coffee service cabinet. Rubbing her lower back, she watched the man at the counter by the name of Ash. He was a poster for tall, dark, and handsome—smoking hot eyes under thick black hair, pensive face with a dash of mystery. *With those looks he should be in a steamy TV series,* she thought. She had never fallen for a man, but she could see herself ... maybe ... falling for someone like this one.

Checking on the other counter customer, and a booth of three, Star swung back by Ash who was still nursing his coffee. Topping off his mug, she tilted her head. "You said you'd take any job but if you had a choice, what would it be?"

"Maybe a cook," he said with a slight curve to his lips nodding at Jonny behind the order window.

"I'm a pastry chef, or was," Star said. "A cook's position is pretty much filled now, but the turnover is constant here at the beach, not for chefs but short-order cooks. You have to be in the right place at the right time. I picked up this job last week. Needed something quick ... a long sordid story." Star grimaced. "Take a walk down the street, both sides, pop in, ask if they need help. You might strike it lucky like I did. Stop back later. Tell me how it went ... that is if you want to. I'm pretty familiar with some of the places. Don't count out starting as a waiter."

Tyler came in early, asked Star if there was anything he should be aware of about the likes, dislikes of the customers seated on his side of the diner. Star told him everything was under control. She had the two men sitting at opposite ends of the counter. Star rang up the register giving a woman, an infant in her arms, her change.

Feeling a sharp elbow in her back, she turned to Ty.

"That guy at the counter. Know him?"

"No, just making conversation. He's looking for summer work."

Ty left her, introducing himself to a new group in booth one—"cream, sugar, maybe ketchup?" Hustling to the order window, he picked up four plates of pancakes, lining them up his arm, a pitcher of syrup swinging from his little finger at the end of the row of plates.

• • •

THE FEW EARLY-MORNING regulars sauntered out, replaced by late-morning tourists preparing for a frolic on the beach across the street, perhaps the boardwalk down by the Ferris wheel, or rollercoaster. One couple fed the old Wurlitzer with more than a few quarters playing one movie soundtrack over and over, *The Sting*, rocking the walls of the diner for almost an hour. The red, purple, and blue neon circling the ceiling jumped gaily in rhythm to the music.

Wanda nodded to Star. “How about a cup of coffee? Take advantage of a slow spell before the sunbathers return, burnt to a crisp. Give you and me a chance to talk.”

Star let a puff of air roll over her lips. A chance to get off her feet, even for a few minutes, was an invitation not to be passed up. Smoothing her black apron over her short black skirt, she slid into the booth across from Wanda, a cup of coffee waiting for her. Ty was quick where Star was concerned, Wanda too, of course.

“What do you think so far?” Wanda asked looking over the top of her mug at Star. “I have to say, I’ve never seen anyone adapt to a situation as fast as you.”

“You’re not as surprised as I am. I’m amazed at how I begin to see the regulars as real people, a peek into their lives.”

“Anyone particular?”

“Yes … the Butterworth sisters are priceless. And, Benny is a hoot. Has he ever told you what happened, why he’s in a wheelchair?”

“No, he hasn’t. Maybe some kind of accident. The war … always a war somewhere it seems.”

“Wanda, I love it here. Before, I was so busy in the kitchen I missed everything that was going on out front. Very important to see how, and more important, *if* your customers are enjoying their food.”

“But at the Manatee you were out front.”

“Well … yes, but serving drinks was much different. Had to dodge some of the more aggressive men, if you know what I mean.”

“A pretty girl like you? I can only imagine.”

“Excuse me, Wanda. The man coming in the door was here this morning, new to the area. I’ll—”

Wanda’s head jerked up. “Wait. You smell that? Something’s burning.”

Star glanced over at the order window as she stood up, a swirl of smoke curling up to the tin ceiling.

Charlie stormed out of the diner's tiny back office. In three strides he was standing nose to nose in front of Jonny, yelling at Jonny tossing three charred burgers into the trashcan beside the grill. Charlie's eyes bulged, temples throbbing as he looked down at the burgers lying in the trash. "What's the matter with you? Not just burning ... incinerating burgers? And, the man in booth four this morning wanted hash browns, not burnt hash, burnt hash to go with the eggs scrambled ... not over-easy."

"Nothing's the matter with me. It's that new waitress. I can't read her writing."

"Yeah? I think you're stoned. What do you say to that?"

"I quit. That's what I say to that." Jonny yanked off the bib apron stained with egg yolks and bacon grease. "I'll be back tomorrow for my pay."

"Oh, no. I don't want to see your sour face again. Wanda, get the man a twenty."

Wanda hustled to the counter, pulled a twenty out of the register shoving the bill against Jonny's chest.

"Okay, now git," Charlie snapped, glaring at the man passing himself off as a cook.

"Twenty? You owe me more than twenty."

"Let's just call it even after all the food you wasted, not to mention what you've stuffed into that oversized gut of yours. Oh, yeah, I caught you plenty of times. Out!"

Charlie stood, hands on his hips, fuming, knowing it meant more hours he didn't have to spare, or the strength to stand at the grill. A family slid into an empty booth, laughing, brushing off the itchy salt sticking to their legs from the surf. Now, what was he going to do?

Good riddance, Star thought. The jerk didn't fit in. Charlie and Wanda are too good for him. No wonder customers are going someplace else.

Ash, sitting at the counter watched the banished cook slam out the side door. Others looked around at the altercation, watching Charlie, wondering if they were going to get the lunch they ordered.

Ash squinted, then stood and walked around the corner of the counter.

Charlie's brows hitched up wondering what this guy wanted.

"Sir, I can help. I've done some short-order cooking, and—" He backed away as Star popped up in front of him.

"Charlie, I can do it. I can cook. Give me a try ... at least for the day. I'll cook 'til closing. Please. Please." Star edged out Ash, and now stood within five inches of Charlie.

"Give her a try, Charlie," Wanda said with a sigh. "We won't have many customers for the rest of the ... unfortunately, for the rest of the day," she added in a whisper.

Charlie's shoulders slumped, his eyes wearily seeking his wife's, weighing his options. "Two women. I don't have a chance. The grocer called. Our order is packed, ready for me to pick up at the market. I have to go. Wanda, show Star around the grill, the freezer, the pantry. Tyler's here, so I guess it's up to the three of you to keep the place going. I'll hurry."

Four days and she was already a cook. Maybe not a chef, and burgers were not petit fours, but it was a step up in Star's mind.

A sudden guilty feeling swamped over her. She'd been rude, jumping in front of Ash. Picking up the pot of coffee, she approached him.

"Ash, I'm sorry, it's just—"

"Hey, no problem. I worked in the school cafeteria, saw an opportunity to help."

Star topped off his coffee. "See, I really need this job. Charlie's had problems with cooks, so I thought it was a chance to secure my place—"

"It's okay, really. But I see you're not just a pretty blonde with big blue eyes and a soft voice ... that voice comes on strong if something is important to you. A spine of steel I bet. Besides you already have a job here. Seniority."

"Did you have any luck ... a job?"

"Some. I have an interview next week."

"Where?"

"I'll stop by, tell you if I get it." Ash reached into his pocket for change.

"No, no. My treat." Star put her hand up.

"Thanks. See you." Ash slid off the stool, ambled to the door.

"Bye," Star called out.

• • •

AS PROMISED, Charlie hustled in the back door in less than an hour. He and Wanda carted the bags of groceries in from the diner's white, beat-up Ford van, Wanda prattling in his ear every step of the way. "Star is a whiz, Charlie. Encourage her to take on the dinner service. You look exhausted."

Over the next two hours there was a burst of activity—two booths, a table of three, and four of the counter stools turned over. The scent of coconut sun-screen over-rode burgers and bacon. Sunburned, exhausted beach bunnies straggled in and straggled out.

The day had flown by. Hands hanging by his side, Charlie shook his head at Wanda slouching on a chair opposite Ty.

Tyler was hunched over the table, scribbling, or drawing with quick, broad strokes on the back of one of the diner's paper placemats. He grabbed a second placemat, then a third, his hand repeating the gyrations, stopping only for a second when he saw Star. She had finished scraping and scouring the grill. She strolled out from behind the order window—whistling.

Sliding along the red-vinyl bench next to Tyler, the toes on one foot pushing off a white sneaker, then, switching feet, pushed off the other sneaker.

Charlie shook his head again—the woman was whistling. He shuffled to lock the side door then the front door wondering at Star's stamina. After what had gone on today, he could barely manage to lock up, let alone pucker his lips to whistle. How did she do it?

Charlie leaned against the old Wurlitzer. "Star, if you want a job as our cook just say the word. I don't know where you came from or where you're going, but as long as you're here, we'd like you to be our cook. I'll take the early morning shift. You start with the lunch crowd to closing."

"I'd like that." Star grinned at Charlie, then Wanda. Wiggling her toes, she slipped on her sneakers. "Charlie, mind if Ty and I grab a coke? Thought we might take a walk down to the beach. That is if you don't have plans, Ty? I promise I won't talk your ears off—work talk. We both have to get some sleep."

"Hey, you two go right ahead. Tomorrow's Friday, payday. Consider the coke on the house."

"Thanks, Charlie." Ty carefully stacked the three menus he had scribbled on, folded them in half, in half again, and a final fold sliding them in his pocket and scampered out the back door after Star.

Chapter 3

"FEEL THE AIR, Ty. Isn't it glorious?" Star was already across the street, calling to him, waving her arms over her head, dancing around, touching her toes, laughing at Ty's gangly gait hustling across the street to join her.

Catching her infectious laughter, a smile filled his face, chuckling at her dancing.

Shouldering her tote she grabbed his hand, pulling him down the path between the shops to the beach. Skidding to a stop a few feet from the waves, she drew open the tote, dug out her white bib apron spreading it on the sand. Dropping cross legged, she patted the apron for him to sit. Tyler in an awkward movement, his legs not cooperating, sat beside her leaning back on his elbows.

Star looked up at the blanket of stars reaching to the horizon, fading away in the bright lights of the Ferris wheel and boardwalk along the midway behind her. It was a night to be out, out enjoying the cool breeze pushing away the heat and humidity of the afternoon. Screams from riders braving the rollercoaster mixed with the jingle of the pinball machines in the arcade, mixed with the squeals of young and old as the surf swirled over bare feet.

Glancing away from the new moon, she observed Tyler twisting the tie of her apron. "Ty, what were you doing with those menus ... just before we left?"

Leaning on one elbow so he could straighten out his body to get into his front pants pocket, he pulled out the folded sheets. "Now, don't laugh."

"I won't. Let me see." Star tried to pluck the sheets from his fingers but he was too quick, pulling them out of her reach. She chuckled. Ty looked like a character off the cover of her Gran's stack of Saturday Evening Post magazines stored in the garage.

"Promise you won't laugh?"

"Promise." She crossed her heart and politely held out her palm to him.

He handed over the folded menus. Hugging his knees, he stared at her face as she slowly unfolded the placemats ... dramatically ... slowly ... glancing at him as each fold opened, nodding at him, squinching her eyes to slits like a Cheshire cat about to discover a hidden treasure.

Carefully smoothing out the creases of the top sheet of three on her lap, her expression changed from Cheshire to shock.

A fresh ocean breeze fluttered the edges as she lifted the top sheet, then the second, to the third. She reshuffled the pages, sorting through them again, grasping them tightly to thwart another breeze from stealing them away.

Star began to laugh, jumping to her feet. She viewed all three again, still laughing. At each page she paused, grinned at Ty, laughter spilling from her lips.

Ty was startled when she flopped beside him, the menus clutched in her hand as she hugged him, then sat back. "Ty, you are an artist. Cartoons? Caricatures? How did you learn? You captured everyone perfectly. Not only do you *look* like Norman Rockwell, you are a direct descendant."

"Well, I wouldn't exactly go that far." He looked up at Star sheepishly, a grin slowly spreading ear to ear. "But you can say it again ... if you want to ... if you really mean it. Do you really like them?"

"I never asked your last name. Tyler Norman Rockwell ... what?"

Tyler rocked, clutching his knees. No one had ever been excited about his work, least of all a girl. Well, Star wasn't any girl. She was a beautiful blue-eyed female ... girl.

Carefully folding the menus, Star handed them back to Ty, then scrunched on the sand, facing him knee to knee. "Spill, Ty."

"Silly, no, my name isn't Norman Rockwell. It's Tyler Randolph Jackman." Again, the sheepish look through the black-rimmed glasses. "Since I was a kid, my classmates laughed at me but, for some reason, I laughed back at them. Of course, I was terrible at sports. Baseball? No way. When I tried to bat I swung so hard that I ended up twirling in a circle. I thought it was funny and because I thought I was funny the kids thought I was funny.

"Tommy Oliver laughed so hard he peed his pants. But, Star, something amazing happened, at least to a goofy kid, I thought it earth shattering—'You should see yourself, Tyler. You're a regular ballerina.' Tommy said that. So, I sat on the bench, pulled my notebook from my book bag, and sketched my ballet move swinging the bat. I signed it Tyler Jackman and gave it to Tommy after practice. Tommy showed it to everyone, and honest to God, Star, they all laughed ... not at me ... at Tyler the cartoon. Tommy folded up the paper and said he was keeping it as a souvenir. It would be worth millions, that's what he said, 'millions' when I created comic books featuring Tyler and Tommy, the sportsmen."

"And did you ... create comic books ... how old were you when this ballet move took place?"

"Twelve. I can't remember when I started drawing ... way before. My parents thought it was cute, but cute doesn't make a living, my mom would say. Mom and Dad wanted me to be an engineer, like the rest of the men in the family."

"Okay, Ty, but why are you here, waiting tables? Where are your parents?"

"My parents live here, twelve minutes away, in Ormond Beach. They wanted me to be an engineer so I went to Boston, took a couple of classes at MIT and then switched to art school—

Massachusetts School of Art and Design. Mainly, I wanted to learn about proportions, angles, different styles. Anyway, one of my professors said I had talent. My older sister, she graduated from Stanford and is working for a high-tech company in Silicon Valley ... she kept encouraging me. Since my sister gave my folks their engineer I felt free to pursue what I wanted. Sylvia, that's my sister, conspired with me to take the art classes. She laughed at my cartoons, just like you, well almost like you. After all, she's my sister. Sometimes a cartoon made her cry."

"Cry?"

"Yeah, like a cartoon of a little guy with big tears rolling down his face, dropping on his shirt because of a ginormous bully. But, you are the first to really get what I was trying to say."

"So, why are you waiting tables in a diner? Don't tell me you're giving up your dream of creating comic books—Tyler and Tommy? *You* have to have top billing—Tyler before Tommy," Star said peering at him.

"No, I haven't given up ... but ... don't laugh. Promise?"

"Promise." Star nodded inching closer, knees now touching.

"My dream is to draw character animations for Disney—"

"That's why you didn't stay in Boston, returned to Florida to be closer to Orlando and Disney World?"

"Kinda ... Disney World is the park, all the animations for their films are produced in studios, like in Burbank. I live with my folks until I land a job in the animation world, the world of make believe. I'm putting together a presentation. I'll store it on a flash drive, or CD ... a disc would be easier to mail. Hmm. I'm compiling a list of companies to submit it to ... maybe to Disney ... maybe not. Definitely not. It would land in the slush pile. I'll have a better chance if I can land a job, get some experience in the field first ... don't you think?"

Star nodded. "I think."

"Should I change my name? Something funny, to catch attention? Garfunkel and Humperdinck are already taken," he said laughing. "So, I came up with Kent, as in Clark Kent, A-K-A Superman. What do you think?"

"I think you should keep your name, your family name. I can see the credits sliding up the screen ... Tyler Jackman, Producer, Director, and Creator. By the way, that cartoon of me cooking—the scrambled eggs did not hit the wall."

"Did too," Ty said grinning.

"Did not."

"I saw them go splat when your chef's hat slipped over your eyes, just before you flipped the French toast into the pot of boiling potatoes. By the way, no kidding, maybe instead of a chef's hat you should try a ball cap—spongy sweat band and a hole in the back for your yellow hair, you know catch the sweat before it blinds you, keep the French toast from flying out the order window."

"I can see perfectly well, thank you," she said punching his arm.

"Yeah, a ball cap would be perfect. Your cerulean-blue eyes peer out from under the visor, see the kid stab a piece of toast with his fork as it flies by from the order window."

"Like I have time to watch toast fly," Star said mocking his suggestion. "Cerulean-blue?"

"Sky blue, azure. Definitely azure—a hint of purple. Seriously, I'm glad the diner's not that busy. I need some time to create."

"Create?"

"Oh, yeah. Catch you in the action. It's hilarious watching you whip and flip and pinch spices."

Star giggled. "I think you'll be a big, successful cartoonist, Tyler Jackman. You see humor everywhere."

"Good, just like I know you'll be famous someday ... Rachael Ray famous. Martha Stewart famous. No, no, Julia Child famous. She was a spy you know."

Chapter 4

FLIP. FLIP. FLIP.

Star chuckled thinking of Ty's cartoons of her flipping pancakes lined up across the grill. The egg beater spewing yokes against the wall, specks of mashed potato flung from the whisk onto her nose, and grease—bacon, sausage, and burgers—dotting the front of her white bib apron.

He had captured her blue eyes—wide, astonished at a pancake flying through the air. The white billowing chef's hat, she insisted on wearing, giving the order window certain panache as it slipped to the side revealing springy curls.

The cartoons were crazy-fun illustrations of her life. Taking Ty's idea of a ball cap, she made it a point to stop by the T-shirt shop next door to the diner. After trying on a few, she picked up a visor with a dark red bill, a rainbow arching over a yellowish-orange sun. Checking her image in the makeshift mirror, the shiny chrome upright of the jewelry display case, she decided the visor would do nicely—moisture wicking sweatband anchoring her hair from falling in her eyes. Not a full-fledged baseball cap to pull her ponytail through, just the bill. Much lighter, letting her scalp breathe. Heaven knows, she needed all the air she could get hunching over the hot grill.

It was time to retire the chef's hat, at least for the summer.

Happy with the look, she purchased the visor wearing it out into the sunshine, hustling back to the diner. Sidling up to Ty, she struck a pose, batting her eyelashes. He was leaning against the coffee station, sketching on a paper tablet, pretending to be oblivious to her antics. Peeking around his arm, Star gave him a punch, giggling at his cartoon of an olive-skinned man, Ash, perched on what had become *his* seat at the end of the counter.

"I see you, missy. Here, take a look at this." Ty flipped back a few pages, showing her a cartoon of Benny trying to fit his wheelchair under the edge of *his* bistro table.

With a smile at Ty, Star relieved Charlie behind the grill finishing the breakfast order for the Butterworth sisters in booth one. Tyler closed his pad, slipping it behind a stand of mustard and ketchup bottles, and picked up the plates of eggs, sausage, hash browns, with a side of six pancakes. Swinging a syrup pitcher from his little finger, he nodded at Star as she tilted her head in a salute, her fingers touching the bill of her new visor.

"Yeah, nice hat, sorta hat. Are you always so cheerful?"

"I'm pretending, sir. You see me scrambling eggs. I see me gently whipping cream to the perfect consistency for a delicate tiramisu."

"Hmm. Pretending?" Turning, he quickly took off for booth one.

The Butterworth sisters were regulars, every Wednesday morning like clockwork chattering enthusiastically, arriving for breakfast and almost always wearing a new T-shirt proclaiming their latest adventure.

Mattie and Hattie sitting across from Anne, the eldest sister and their leader, beamed at Ty as he positioned their breakfast plates in front of them. Mattie and Hattie giggled, elbowing each other, gray mops of curls around apple cheeks, their T-shirts stretched over their ample bodies—*Happy Dieter*.

The Happy Dieters carefully dissected the sausage, buttered the pancakes, and kept their forks performing the *quick step* between plate and mouth as they exchanged opinions on the wafer-thin instructor of their new line-dancing class. A class guaranteed to get you in shape for the beach wearing a new teeny-weeny bikini. Mattie said she enjoyed the new dance steps, especially the country music. But Hattie thought the bikini thingy wasn't going to happen in her lifetime. Taking a stab at a piece of sausage, Anne waved at Tyler to get his attention.

"Miss Butterworth, what can I get for you?"

"Tyler dear, can you ask Star to come over when she has a minute? We have a question for her."

Her sisters energetically nodded in agreement.

"Of course, and I'll top off that coffee."

Stepping lively, Ty whispered to Star, stopped to pick up the pot of coffee and followed Star to the sisters.

Anne's face intensely earnest looked up at Star. "Star dear, my sisters and I detect a certain new taste in the pancakes this morning. Something different."

"Is it different good or different bad?" Star asked, finger to her cheek in feigned concern.

"Definitely good. Good, wouldn't you say, Mattie?"

"Yes, definitely good," Mattie and Hattie chirped.

Leaning in, a conspiratorial look on her face, Star whispered, "Just a dash, mind you."

"What, what?"

"Nutmeg!"

Nodding, Ty quickly retrieved his tablet from the ketchup and mustard, capturing the sisters as they polished off the last of the nutmeg pancakes before leaving for their line-dance class.

Chapter 5

YANKING HER BICYCLE out of her apartment, Star closed and locked the door behind her. The only door, unless she considered the slider to a small patio a door. She adjusted the basket on the handlebars and the one strapped to the back of the bike's seat.

Pedaling off she felt the advent of summer's sun on her bare legs and arms. It was good to be away from the heat of the grill. Her white shorts and blue tank top were light as opposed to the bib apron's heavy cotton. Raising her chin to the soft ocean breeze, inhaling the salty air, she pedaled faster.

Adjusting her visor, which had now become the last thing she tugged in place whenever she went out, she headed for the T-shirt store to buy seven more, one for each day of the week and one extra when the others hit the washing machine. She dubbed the sweatband one of the greatest inventions, keeping the sweat from running into her eyes as she darted around the tiny space behind the grill that Wanda called a kitchen.

It was Star's day off and she had errands to run—a list of spices to pick up for the diner and a few for her own so-called pantry.

Her empty backpack didn't move as she cruised down Atlantic Avenue. Squinting from the sun unless she kept her head down, she swung up to the bicycle rack by the door to the shop almost running into Ash standing on the sidewalk to the side of the entrance. He was bent over writing something on a yellow notepad propped against his knee. Hearing a bicycle, he jumped back in the nick of time.

"Hey, Ash, sorry. I didn't mean to startle you. You're out early. Whatcha doing?" she said chaining her bike to the stand then lighting up a smile for him.

He nodded to her. "You, too. What's the hurry?"

"My day off and I have a ton of things to do. I'm running in here for some more of these visors. If you have time, how about grabbing a coffee at the 7-Eleven? We can scoot down to the beach for a few minutes. I'd like to hear how your job hunting is going."

"Well ... yeah, okay. You get your visors, and I'll go pick up your coffee. Put anything in it?"

"Black, high test. I'll meet you out front."

Picking up two foam cups of coffee, Ash met up with Star outside the T-shirt shop. Her new visors tucked neatly in her backpack, she nodded for him to follow. Guiding her bike through the path to the beach, she leaned it against the bench attached to the old boards of the boardwalk facing the ocean, the brilliant rays of the sun sparking off the white caps.

Opening the spout of the cup, she sampled a small sip of the hot coffee. "Umm. I needed this. How much do I owe you?"

"My treat."

"Thanks. So, Ash, did you find a job? I've seen you sitting at the counter around lunchtime but I couldn't get away from the grill," she said experiencing a slight hitch in her breathing. It was the first time they sat side by side. Her arm grazed his as she leaned over to brush sand from the top of her sneakers.

"I think so ... yes, yes, I did. At the News Journal as a reporter, a cub reporter I think the Human Resource person labeled it."

Hmm. He seems to be a little nervous around me. Could I be making him nervous? Or, label that wishful thinking. "That's wonderful. I didn't know you were interested in being a reporter."

"Neither did I, I mean I did but, well. See, I'm finishing up at Stetson University in Deland. You've probably heard of it."

"Oh, yes. It's a wonderful school. You're finishing? I thought you said you had finished."

"Yes, I meant I will g- g-graduate in a couple of months. I have one last paper to submit."

I am making him nervous. "You'll receive your degree in what?"

"My major is Communications, finishing up a Master's in Media Services."

"... so ... a job as a reporter is perfect. Congratulations. What, now? You're still looking for a job, or are you independently wealthy? Your parents—"

"No help from my parents. In fact, they are not pleased. But my grandmother believes in me. She lives in London. I wish you could meet her. I'm kind of a wayward child in my family."

His grandmother. As soon as he mentioned her he seemed to relax. "Well, I can understand that. Talking about my parents flusters me more than I like to admit."

"Tell me about it. I'm practically disowned. My family is in Hoboken. Dad is now head of the family business—financial management. I was supposed to be an accountant before I ran down here, literally ran away. My grandmother also believes in me. I came down to Daytona Beach with her taffy recipe. I was going to take the beach concessions by storm, then the world, with her taffy." Star sighed, looking out at the water. "The world ... and now I'm a short-order cook but ... some day."

Star glanced sideways at him, peeking out from under the bill of her visor. His eyes were a beautiful shade of brown, large, friendly when he looked at her. But she saw them turn black when looking in another direction, at others, like he was sizing them up. They sat quietly watching the surf, the sunbathers, children building sandcastles. Comfortable in their own thoughts. Star kept glancing at him out of the corner of her eye as she sipped her coffee.

There was a ruggedness about him accentuated with a heavy shadow of a beard, a scar from his ear to his jaw on the left side. She hadn't noticed it before. She had never seen him clean shaven at the diner, always with a shadow around his chin, upper lip. His body always seemed tense, ready to spring. He never wore shorts like other men, the tourists in shorts or cutoffs. Ash wore leather shoes or sneakers. No flip-flops.

Did she pick up on an accent when he spoke? There was something about his speech pattern. However, there was nothing wrong with his smile when he looked at her. It was soft, warm. Did he feel something, too?

"What, what? Did you say something?" She turned responding to his voice.

His lips parted, a slight grin crossing his face. "I asked if you ever sold any of your grandmother's taffy—the shops behind us?"

"I tried for a week or two. One of the booths was vacated and the manager of the space, I had met him before, gave him my phone number if anything opened it ... anyway, he called. It was horrible. I had to man the booth for twelve hours, make the taffy at night, up the next morning to hurry down here to the booth. I couldn't do it. Sure was a lesson in how *not* to run a business."

Ash leaned back, crossed his legs, laying his hands on his thighs the sun warming his face.

Star looked at his hands. They were smooth, no construction for this man. She wanted to touch one, but something in his manner said not to. Whatever he did before going to school at Stetson had made his body rock hard. "What do your parents do?" She assumed they lived in England along with his grandmother.

"My mother stayed at home. My father is in the army."

"Hmm. Did you move around? The military?"

"No."

Sensing he didn't want to talk about his parents, Star asked how he liked being a reporter. He relaxed, and at the same time seemed excited chatting about his assignments, submitting them for print. No byline—yet. For the most part the assignments had been fun—a gator in a community pond, a bear cub up a tree.

They glanced up at a group of children running with kite strings clutched in their hands. Not looking where they were going, they scattered sand on Star's bare legs, on Ash's pant legs. Brushing the sand away, they both laughed. Star touched his hand. She didn't mean to, it was a natural friendly gesture, friends responding to the sand kicked up by the children. His laugh trailed off. Ash didn't move, didn't touch her pale hand on his olive skin. The tension between them was magnetic.

Standing up, she smiled at him. He immediately rose to his feet. His eyes were warm again looking into her eyes. Her breathing took another hitch. *I wonder if he feels the same connection. He didn't sit close to me on the bench, could have, but didn't. We didn't touch except when I brushed at the sand.* "Thanks again, Ash, for the coffee. I have to get on with my errands."

"Me too. I have a story to finish for Saturday's paper. Maybe we can meet for coffee again."

"I'd like that."

She shouldn't have done it, but she did. She leaned in and kissed his cheek. "Bye."

She could feel his warm eyes following her as she walked her bike back up the path to the street.

Chapter 6

SPICE UP THE DINER'S MENU, that's what she had to do. Create excitement.

"Bite size meatballs—sausage or beef—call them meatball tarts or tartlets. Offer them on the breakfast, lunch, and dinner menu."

Wanda and Charlie didn't know what to make of Star's idea. Traffic was down. Charlie threw his hands in the air. "Go ahead ... run with it."

Star exchanged a grin with Tyler and set to work experimenting with a spicy chili sauce for the more adventuresome diner. Wiping her hands on a paper towel, shoulders slumping, she was flummoxed over the growing list of items missing from the cabinets.

And, she needed a car.

With a growing list on two sheets of her pink pad of paper, she approached Wanda, convincing her that most of the utensils, pans, and a mixer could be found at Wal-Mart, or Big Lots. If she was going to be the diner's cook, then she required some real chef equipment. With Wanda's nudging, Charlie agreed Star could buy a few things, but he thought several items on the list were frivolous—the others he would pay for, and yes, she could borrow the diner's van.

Tyler, standing behind her when she spoke with Charlie, immediately chimed in that he wanted to go along—to help carry everything, to be a spotter for the list of items on the pink pad, to make the excursion more expeditious.

Wanda quickly agreed to switching shifts with Tyler, but called out urging him not to be gone too long as he backed the van out of the reserved parking spot behind the diner.

At their first stop, Wal-Mart, Ty commandeered a shopping cart from the greeter and proceeded to whiz down the aisles following in Star's wake, but when she paused to read a descriptive label, he pulled out his pad from under his shirt, sketching furiously. Star peeked at his work and laughed at the cartoons of an impish blonde cook. If she was ever going to publish a cookbook she knew who to ask for a raft of illustrations.

The one item she really wanted she hadn't been able to find. So she called Pier 1 on her cell phone, ending an animated conversation with a fist pump and a smile at Ty. "Come on. We have one more stop. If the pot rack at Pier 1 isn't exactly what I want then I'll order it online."

Sliding onto the front seat next to Ty, she began scratching off the items she had found, circled ones she didn't find, and firmed up her *to-do* list for tomorrow.

"Ty, I'm going to present a new menu to Charlie and Wanda. Can I use some of your cartoons?"

"Thought you'd never ask. Sounds fun." Watching her, his heart became squirrelly in his chest. She was so damn cute and she finally asked him for help. It was fun to draw her and the more he drew the more he felt adrenalin coursing through his body, or was it something else. She filled his last thoughts at night when he turned off the light by his bed, and darn it he also woke up thinking about her. Use his cartoons? He'd do anything for her.

"Maybe we could put up a few in the diner. You could sign them... like a renowned cartoonist," She said, head bent adding another item to the list. "Wouldn't that be something if Mr. Disney walked in?" she said glancing up, her blue eyes wide, brows arched.

"Yeah, especially since it would be his ghost. He would freak everyone out."

They laughed as Ty turned onto International Speedway heading to Pier 1. Luckily, they had one pot rack left. Star was so excited she hugged Tyler. He thought for sure his knees would buckle as he hugged her back, wondering if she was this excited about a pot rack, what would she do with something really big.

Back in the parking spot at the rear of the diner, they hustled, making several trips, carting the items she purchased, essential she told Charlie with a wink, to create a working kitchen, albeit tiny.

Ty screwed bolts into the ceiling, clipping on the chains to hold the pot rack. Charlie stood at the grill to be sure the rack was high enough so it wouldn't strike his head, but low enough so Star could reach the pots and whatever else she was going to hang off it. She didn't buy any grill utensils. What spatulas, forks, and tongs Charlie had would do. But the spices, a few molds, and plastic bins of all sizes were new. The bins were critical to keep the limited space organized.

Relieving Charlie, Star chatted with the owners as she placed the various items in arms reach no matter how she turned, then immediately set to work with her new menu items: bite size meatball and sausage tartlets with a special sauce.

She explained how they would be served as she stirred the pureed mixture. One pot with a thick tomato sauce divided in half into a second pot. In the second she added red-pepper flakes, and a dash of chili powder. With a spoon she held up a taste to Wanda's lips, then Charlie's lips watching for their reaction. Their eyes popped, followed by a broad smile. She was onto something. Unwrapping ten pounds of fresh hamburger she'd selected at Wal-Mart, she added several spices, formed the meat into thumb-size balls. Lining the balls on a sheet pan, a quick shake of pepper, garlic salt, and a drizzle of olive oil, she slid the mini-balls into the oven.

For the first batch of tartlets, she bought prepared small filo pastry shells. Checking the oven—baking, then crisping up the surface of the meat—she turned to the sauce.

An idea hit her.

A cranberry glaze with a few drops of hot sauce to give a surprise zip of heat on the tongue.

Wanda stood on the outside of the order window, forearms resting on the high counter, waiting. The aroma of the meatball tartlets circled the diner.

Tyler created a sign: Today's lunch special: *Meatball mini-tarts*. Curving down the left side was a cartoon of Star, serving up a plate of three meatball tarts with cranberry sauce. The perky cook with curls was grinning from ear to ear, her white chef coat dotted with cranberries.

Star swapped baking sheets, sliding the mini filo-dough tarts into the oven for a three-minute warm-up. Working quickly, she constructed the mini tarts—a mini meatball into the mini tart with a dollop of sauce. Sampling the three sauces, brows scrunched in concentration, she let the flavors slide over her pallet.

The taste wasn't quite right. Missing something. It was time for another opinion.

She plated three servings, two tarts on each plate. Then quickly put samples of the sauces into two ramekin dishes—thick tomato with pepper flakes and chili powder, and whole-berry cranberry glaze with hot sauce.

Star served Charlie, Wanda, and Ty sitting in booth number one, waiting patiently to perform a taste test.

Not saying a word, they spooned a small amount of each sauce on the tarts. Picking up the knife and fork, the tasters carefully cut off small bites. The visiting gourmet reporters closed their eyes.

Charlie's eyes popped wide first, grabbing a glass of ice water. "Good, but I hit a clump of pepper flakes. Not quite ready for prime time."

Wanda was next. Looking from her husband to Star. "I love it. And the addition of meat mini-tarts on the new menu will spark conversation. I mean, whoever heard of meatball tartlets with cranberries?" she asked with a little grin.

Ty had quickly polished off his serving. "I think they're great. How about another sauce with a sesame-ginger flavor or would that be too B-B-Quey?"

"I'll give it a try. Thank you all. It's back to my laboratory." Star smiled at Ty who picked up the clean plates with only a small smear of sauce left on each.

Chapter 7

BUSHED, READY TO CALL IT A DAY, Ash sauntered in and sat on his counter stool waiting for Star to finish cleaning up the grill.

Scowling, Tyler turned his back to Ash. It seemed Ash was always walking Star home.

Ty didn't have a chance. He thought maybe he could catch her in the morning, walk her to work. But no, Ash was already waiting on the sidewalk with an extra foam cup of hot chocolate. Seemed Star now preferred the taste of chocolate first thing to start her day, letting his diner coffee carry her through the rest of the shift.

Ty looked at the three cartoons on the wall he had drawn of Star cooking up her special meatball mini-tarts. She had mounted them in black frames with red matting, showing off the black and white pen drawings. Turning, he watched Star leave ... smiling up at Ash ... laughing at something he said.

Ash held the diner's door open for her as she stepped out into the balmy night air. The heat of the day had cooled considerably, but it was still in the eighties and still humid. All Star knew was that the air felt good on her smooth skin, each pore coming alive. Walking down the handicap ramp to the sidewalk, they were close, so close she could feel the warmth of him. Her arm brushed against his arm. She didn't move away.

At the stoplight, he picked up her hand as they crossed the street. Electricity shot through her body—to her heart, stomach, and beyond.

Without looking at her, sauntering along, Ash brought her hand to his lips, to his cheek, continued walking, still holding her hand, arms swaying in rhythm between them. "How was your day?" he asked.

Star looked up, his warm eyes seeking hers. "I had a good day. Actually, quite good. Bought some spices ... now don't laugh."

He smiled. "I won't laugh. What kind of spices?"

"Chili powder, red pepper flakes, and some nutmeg. I ran out of nutmeg. It's a new item—pancakes with just a pinch of nutmeg."

"I see. I don't believe I've ever tasted nutmeg pancakes."

"How was your day, Ash?" She loved to say his name. "Any assignments? New stories? Interviews?" The words came out in spurts. She was embarrassed. He must think she's a star-struck school girl, not a woman who wanted more time with him—more, more, more time.

"Ah, stories. A couple. I have to write them up tonight. Submit them in the morning."

"When will they be in the paper? I'd like to read them. Will you have a by-line?"

His laugh was soft, more of a chuckle. "Not yet. But someday I will ... have a byline."

Even though they were walking, even though he was only holding her hand, Star felt the mere holding of her hand was like he was making love to her. There was so much she wanted to know about him but right now just being close, walking, under the biggest moon she'd ever seen, and the warm air caressing them, she could hardly breathe. Breathing might interrupt the feeling, the electricity sparking between them. Surely he felt it. Of course, he did. He kissed the top of her hand, held it to his cheek. She felt the bristles of his beard. His thumb slowly moved over her skin.

They turned down the street to her building. To her front door.

She turned, faced him, their eyes looking deep into each other's core. Ash put his hands on her cheeks, his fingers moving for a second on the silky skin of her face. He lowered his lips to hers, his lips brushing softly across her full, plump lips. "I'm glad you had a good day, Star. You work hard. You deserve it. You deserve every day to be good. I'll be on the corner in the morning."

Star unlocked her door fumbling with her key. She turned, he was standing on the sidewalk watching, watching to be sure she was safely inside.

"Goodnight," she whispered.

Ash tipped his head slightly, as she closed the door. With his hands at his side, he ambled up the sidewalk into the starry night.

Chapter 8

A PORTLY WOMAN, bouffant silver hair with a decided pink tint, strutted in the front door of the diner. Large, red cabbage roses scattered here and there over her vivid purple dress, danced merrily with each step. She was followed closely by a vivid, curly red-haired woman, and a handsome Hispanic man.

The redhead giggled, fished a coin out of her purse and fed the Wurlitzer as the others moved on to a booth. She pushed *C3* and with a couple of clicks Scottie McCreery filled the dinner with his country hit, "Feeling it." The man escorted the pink-haired senior lady to a booth, knowing his wife, after selecting a song, would dance her way to him. Playing his cards right, he'd also receive a peck on his cheek.

Grinning to welcome his new guests, cartoons performing handsprings through his head, Tyler walked up to the threesome as they settled in the booth.

"Good morning. New to Charlie's I bet. Can I get you some coffee or—"

"Yes, young man," the pink-haired lady said peering over her wire-rimmed spectacles. "Coffee for my niece and her husband, and I think I'll go for a hot chocolate this morning. Whipped cream on top and do you have any of those delightful chocolate sprinkles?" The lady, her hot pink lips bowed, brows raised, waited for Tyler's answer.

"Yes, ma'am, you bet we do." The grin remained on his face, a lovely woman with pink hair frolicking through his mind.

"Jane, Liz, Manny. I don't believe it." Star, vigorously scrubbing her hands on her white cook's apron dotted with bacon grease, appeared at Tyler's side. Her eyes bright, she bent over hugging the pink-haired lady as Liz popped up, arms outstretched, red curls sparking, ready to receive the next hug. Manny also stood, even though he was constrained to move out of the booth as he was next to the window, and stuck out his hand pumping Star's enthusiastically.

"Tyler, please meet three wonderful people. Jane Haliday—"

"That would be me, Tyler." Jane bobbed her head, a smile spreading under her apple cheeks. "This is all just so delightful."

"... and Elizabeth Stitchway and Manny Salinas."

"Make that Elizabeth Stitchway Salinas," the red-haired woman sang out. "Manny and I were married last year."

"Oh, congratulations." Star wrapped Liz in a second tight squeeze.

"Wait," Tyler said, waving two palms in the air. "Are you the Stitchway and Salinas I saw in a newspaper article ... you two forming a Private Detective Agency?" Tyler, not believing his good luck, stared slack-jawed at Manny as a whole new set of cartoons pinged his brain. He was torn between grabbing his sketchpad and talking to his next two characters—maybe even a whole new comic strip.

"That's right, Tyler, Stitch and I—"

"Excuse me, Stitch?"

"Short for Stitchway, Tyler, and—"

"Wait, wait." Star threaded her hand through Tyler's arm. "Everybody, I'd like you to meet Tyler Jackman. See those cartoons." Star pointed across the aisle to the three cartoons of her cooking up the first batch of meatball mini-tarts.

"Oh, how clever. But isn't that you, Star?" Jane asked giving Tyler the once over.

"The diner's cook walked out and I stepped in. Not quite a pastry chef, but at least I'm cooking—short-order cook ... for at least the summer."

"But what about the pastry chef? You had a job."

"Jane, it's a terrible story." Star felt a stab of failure at the question ... *Jane is thinking she'd wasted money on financing my culinary school classes.*

"Okay, you're having way too much fun over here. Relatives, Star?" Charlie asked.

"Oh, better than relatives," she responded. "Charlie, please meet my personal benefactor, Jane Haliday, and my special friends Liz and Manny."

"Welcome to our diner. Benefactor?"

"It's a wonderful story. I'll fill you in later."

"Let me tell you the story right now, Charlie. This honest woman found something of mine, a priceless possession, which she returned to me. Not many would have been so honest." Jane reached up, patted Star's arm.

Tyler remained rooted to the black and white checkered floor, adding another two frames to the comic strip.

Charlie glanced around. "It's a little slow, Star. Why don't you sit with your friends? We can handle their order ... can't we Tyler?"

"You bet, Charlie. I'm off to get two cups of coffee and a hot chocolate with sprinkles ... our most tasty chocolate sprinkles."

"Thanks, Charlie," Star said untying her apron and sliding into the booth next to Jane.

Tyler rocked up on his toes, beaming at Star. For once he could serve her. He handed his guests a menu and then scurried off for the coffees and hot chocolate.

"What a nice young man. And, Star, I think he has an eye for you."

"Oh, Jane, I don't think so. But, we are good friends."

"If you say so, dear."

Star nodded to Jane in agreement. "Charlie makes great omelets, and pancakes, and ... everything."

Tyler arrived with a tray, placing two coffees in front of his private detectives. With a slight bow to Jane he set her hot chocolate on the table along with a grin, and then a bow to Star who giggled at his antics serving her coffee.

"Now, favorite people of Star's, what would you like for breakfast?"

Jane laughed at the lanky lad, his pencil poised over his order pad expectantly. He reminded her of someone, but she couldn't come up with a name.

Jane ordered an omelet with a muffin. Liz scrambled eggs with a piece of whole wheat toast.

"How would you like that toast, miss? Light? Medium? Charred?" Tyler asked his face serious, but eyes twinkling.

Liz, a finger to her cheek, thinking. "Make that medium, please. I never had such a choice for a piece of toast."

"Good choice. You, Detective Salinas?"

"This item here, written in pen ... the meatball mini-tart."

Tyler shot a glance at Star who winked at him.

"Another good choice. A new specialty found only at Charlie's diner. Introduced in the cartoon up on the wall ... the one Star pointed out."

"Oh, a new specialty. Tyler, can you change my scrambled eggs to a meatball mini-tart?" Liz asked, holding out her palm to her husband. Manny dug out two quarters. Liz slid out around Tyler and headed to the Wurly.

"Me too. Switch my omelet, please." Jane smiled sweetly at Tyler.

"Certainly, coming right up," he said grinning at Star, who shook her head—she was fine with her coffee.

"My, my. Is he always so, so, animated?" Jane asked, a touch of whipped cream on her upper lip.

"Not quite. I think this is a special show for you."

"Now, tell us what happened to your pastry chef job, dear?"

Star looked away, fidgeted with the handle on her coffee mug, sighed, and with pain written across her face, turned on the bench to face Jane. *I have to be honest. This is so embarrassing,*

Jane of all people. The first person who believed in me ... except for Gran. "I was fired for sexual harassment. Can you believe it? It was really the other way around ... but sometimes well, you know ... wrong place, wrong time."

"What stuff and nonsense. Did you fight back?"

"No. The man, barely twenty I think, was the nephew of the head chef. The chef hardly tolerated me any way. Blamed me for everything that went wrong in the kitchen, thanks to his nephew."

"What about your grandmother's taffy? Have you given up?" Liz asked her face drooping, but her foot tapping to the beat of the music she selected, the neon lighting jumping with the music.

"No, just pushed it to the back burner. I grabbed the first job I saw. Summer is the worst time to be looking for a chef's position. Actually, I started here as a waitress but when Charlie's cook left, fired actually, I asked him to give me a chance. He and Wanda are wonderful. Hired me on the spot but I had to promise to stay through the summer. It gets busy, a little wild in fact, on the beach in the summer."

Tyler set the orders of meatball mini-tarts on the table topped with thick tomato sauce, then stepped back waiting for their reaction.

"Hey, I like this. Very good." Manny had devoured the first one and was digging into the second.

"Do you really like them? Ty, can you bring over a little dish of the cranberry glaze?"

"Right away, Miss Bloom."

"I'm experimenting with cranberries. I'd appreciate your input."

Before Manny had time to stab into the third meatball tart, Tyler was back with a plate of three more tarts without sauce, along with a ramekin of the spicy cranberry glaze. Star's eyes switched back and forth watching her friends' reactions as one by one, with ceremony, they tried the sauce.

"Wow!" Liz declared. The cranberry has a bite to it. What's in it?"

"A little cinnamon, allspice, port wine, and a drop or two of hot sauce. Too much?" Star asked leaning forward.

"No, no—perfect. And I love the pastry ... gives a nice crunch." Liz said, nodding to Jane.

"Yes. I believe I like it just as it is. Manny, you?"

Manny gestured to his clean plate, and the empty plate Tyler had brought over for testing. Nodding in agreement. Enough said.

"What can I do to take them from good to better, even best ever?"

"Put them at the top of the menu, dear. Right under one of Tyler's cartoons of you."

Spooning on an extra helping of cranberries, Liz looked up at Star. "What are you going to do? I mean these meatballs are to die for, but your talents lie in pastries, candy, baking."

"I don't know. I'd like to capitalize on my training ... thanks to you, Jane. My months at the hotel were beyond thrilling, that is until ... you know. There's a little shop about a mile from here. They sell souvenirs and are planning to pull out at the end of the summer season when their rental agreement is up. It would make a wonderful little bakery shop. My Gran said she'd put up some seed money for equipment—refrigerator, maybe a gas stove, to say nothing of the mixers, torches to put the finishing touch on crème brûlée ..."

Star stopped rattling on. "But to start a business as an unknown, I'd need more. As I said, my commitment here is until the end of summer. That was the deal with Wanda and Charlie. They're great but, as you said, my dreams lay elsewhere and not as a short-order cook," she whispered.

Manny elbowed Liz. "What about that TV show we saw last night?"

"Oh, that was a hoot. A reality TV bakeoff. Star, there were four women, each had helpers from their bakeries. Anyway, it was a competition. The winner took home a cool seventy-five grand. You could do that. I bet you'd win."

"I don't know. You said they already had bakeries."

Liz reached across the table grasping Star's hand. "They all did. But the host talked about an upcoming series for amateur bakers. I can't remember how much he said the prize money was. Can you, Manny?"

"Only that it was a lot and it was set up to run seven or eight episodes. Google it, Star. We will too. If we find it, we'll email you the link."

"Wow! Do you really think I'd have a chance?"

"I think!" Liz said, her red curls sparking.

Chapter 9

THE REST OF the afternoon sped by. A blur. Star snatched the orders clipped to the wire above the order window, robotically filling them, all the while her mind replaying the visit of her friends. It had been wonderful to see Jane again. Their conversation had stirred up the dreams she had tamped down.

Enter a bakeoff?

She had won a few blue ribbons at the county fair in Hoboken. But a fair was not a bakery business. Maybe a short-order cook was to be her lot in life. *No, no, I want more. The pastry chef at the hotel wasn't a bakery either.* Maybe they did her a favor by firing her. Wake her up, strive for more, shoot higher.

The tartlets had added a bit of humor to the diner's menu, especially with Ty's cartoons. Actually, he brought the menus to life more than she did. She added another item to the menu—mid-size filo-dough shells filled with salad. Mothers exclaimed that it was the first time their children would eat a salad. So salads became a hit, too.

Business was picking up.

It was almost closing time and Ash was waiting for her at the end of the counter. She finished cleaning the grill as Ty finished bussing the tables.

Joining Ash at the counter, leaning on his forearms, he drained his coffee mug. "Long day? You look tired."

"Yes, but it was fun. Some old friends stopped by."

Ty, hearing her mention her friends, sidled over, even though he didn't want to *join them* only her. "What was that about ... you're finding something of Jane's?" he asked.

Sighing, she looked wistfully at the two of them ... thinking back. "Just over a year ago, a twister came through here. It tore up a street in a small community of manufactured homes. Jane's was one of them. But she survived because Morty, her long departed husband, had insisted on a safe room—an iron room bolted to the carport's cement slab. After the twister was gone, Jane emerged from the room to find everything gone—her house, everything in it. Everything including several little people she kept on a holiday tree in her living room, year round. The angel on the top of the tree landed in a bush outside of my studio, same place I live now."

"That had to be several miles away," Tyler said, bending over, his pointy elbows resting on the counter.

"That's right. But this wasn't just any angel. Before Jane's husband died, they had collected precious stones which she pasted as pretty, sparkling decorations to the characters on her tree. When Morty died, Jane put his very large gold wedding band, circled with diamonds, on top of the angel ... a halo. Because of a TV report, I learned Jane was the owner and I returned the angel to her. She was so thankful, she gave me enough money to take a year of culinary classes at Daytona Beach College—the college now connected with Florida State University."

"No wonder the lady with pink hair thinks you are her angel, returning her husband's wedding ring." Tyler looked off, staring blankly at the wall... adding a few more frames to the comic strip triggered earlier.

"Pink-haired lady?" Ash asked.

"You had to be here. See you tomorrow, Star." With a scowl, Ty tossed his apron in the hamper on his way out the back door.

• • •

STEPPING OUT Of the diner, Star paused, drawing in a deep breath of the cool salty air. Ash trotted down to the sidewalk, turned, smiling, held out his hand to her. "Taking in the evening air? Freedom from the hot grill?"

"Yes, you could say that." Joining him they darted across Atlantic Avenue mindful of the traffic. With the ocean over the rise, they kept running re-invigorated by the night air.

"Come on, Ash. I hear drumbeats from the Bandshell. Let's check out who's playing."

Hands up like a prize fighter, Ash kept pace jogging beside her.

In sight of the Bandshell, Star flopped on the beach to catch her breath. The beach was almost covered with blankets alongside the Bandshell to the surf—couples, families, loners listening to the music booming from large speakers out over the crowd, over the waves. A thousand or more—sitting or standing in front of the stage, arms raised—swayed to the music.

Star patted the sand, inviting Ash to sit beside her. "You never said ... how long have you been in Daytona Beach?" she asked kicking off her sneakers, tying the laces together, slipping them around the strap of her tote. "Oh, the cool sand feels good on my burning tired feet. So, how long?"

"A few weeks. A month. First day was the day I saw you at the diner. Of course, I visited several times while I was in school, in Deland. How about you? How long have you been in Daytona Beach?"

"Well, I left school, second year at college. I told you my dad said I should major in accounting, join the family business when I graduated. Ugh! All I wanted to do was make taffy, my Gran's recipe. So I conspired with her, and she gave me some money to come to Daytona Beach. I was one of those spring-breakers. After a few tries to convince one of the vendors on the boardwalk that I was the queen of taffy, he just laughed at me. Can you beat that? Laughed at the queen of taffy? Anyway, I decided I'd better get a job quickly before my meager funds ran out."

"And?"

"And, of course I wanted to be in the food industry."

"And?"

"And, by the end of the day I landed a job at the Manatee Bar and Grill—about eight miles south of here—Ponce Inlet. Traded bags of taffy for pitchers of frosty beer and cocktails with little umbrellas. Very festive. Ever have one of those little umbrella things?"

"Nah, I don't drink."

"Me either ... oh, a glass of wine is nice now and then. So the queen of taffy remained a figment of my imagination, only a dream. That was three years ago."

"I believe you'll do it, Star." Ash turned to her, touched a strand of her hair, gently sweeping it behind her ear. She could feel his warm breath on her cheek. His head began to bend ever so slightly to her. "You are so pretty." He touched her arm, his finger tracing down to her wrist, then dropped his hands to his side. "It's getting late and you've had a big day. Come on. I'll walk the Queen of Taffy home."

Her breathing erratic, Star got to her feet, slipped her shoes on, walked beside him. Why didn't he kiss her ... like before? Did she do something wrong? What changed?

Ash jammed his hands into his pockets as he walked beside her. At her door there was no repeat of the kiss. He said goodnight, watched until she was safely inside her apartment.

• • •

ASH REMAINED ROOTED to the sidewalk, the moon casting his shadow out to his side. What was he thinking? Touching her arm, her hair, the silky blonde strand so soft as he carefully put it behind her ear. If only he could have kissed her again. He could tell by the soft look in her eyes, in the light of the moon, that she wanted him to embrace her, to hold her.

Impossible!

His future did not include a woman, not yet, and definitely not this woman. He knew he had to resist. He had made a pact with his grandmother, that if she saw him through college and a master's degree, in return, he was to become her voice. See that her message was heard. She had pleaded with him to stay the course. It would be hard but she knew he could do it. She believed in him and he wasn't going to let her down.

But what about his feelings, these feelings that stirred whenever he was with Star? Well, he had two more months as a reporter for the News Journal. He would spend as much time with Star as she would give him. Then he would leave.

Turning away from her front door, head bent, fists clenched in his pockets, he walked back to his room at the Crescent Moon motel. He had made a deal with the owner, a reduced rate if he stayed three months. His grandmother agreed that it sounded right plus it gave him a place to park his car, a used Volvo to drive wherever the newspaper sent him for a story.

Chapter 10

WITH THIRTY MINUTES to spare before she was scheduled behind the order window, Star hurried into the diner, waved at Charlie cracking an egg on the grill, and slid into an empty booth. Determination written over her face, she had no time for chitchat.

Opening her tote, she pulled out two sheets of paper she'd printed last night before her head hit the pillow—rules to enter the Amateur Bakeoff Competition, the competition that Liz and Manny had suggested. The heading had rocked her to the core: *Win Fifty Thousand Dollars*.

How could that be? Maybe it was a typo. Reading no further, she had turned off the light, tossed and turned the night hours away, going over again and again what that amount of money would mean. Rent the space down the street for starters.

Willing her nerves to settle, her yellow magic marker poised to highlight the pertinent requirements to enter the competition, Star began the entry process. The introductory paragraph thanked her for her interest, asked if she thought she had what it takes to prepare food in a limited amount of time. There was more but she jumped down to the heading: To enter the competition you must submit the following:

There were four bulleted items: A video, a completed application, a copy of photo ID, and a $200 entry fee. Her eyes locked onto the first item—a video.

Tyler set a mug of coffee beside the papers she was studying just as her fist banged down on the table.

"I can't do this." Her finger traced over the word video as if to magically erase it.

"Do what?" Tyler asked.

"Enter this bakeoff competition." Her head flopped back, hand drew over her forehead, eyes riveted on the neon above.

"Why not?" Ty asked, sliding into the booth.

"I don't know how to do the first thing. Ty, the very first thing is to submit a video. No way I can do that. And, I don't have the money to hire someone to shoot a video of me. And, I certainly don't have a kitchen, and ..."

Ty turned the paper around so he could read for himself exactly what they wanted.

"Holy cow. The prize money! Did you see that?"

"Yes. I could hardly miss the big bold print: **WIN FIFTY THOUSAND DOLLARS**. I thought it was a typo."

"There's big money to be made in television, Miss Bloom."

"Ty, read the rules. Submit a video! Fifty grand? Not."

Ty pushed his glasses back up on the bridge of his nose, his eyes darting over the pages.

The rules were explicit. They wanted a video of the entrant preparing an item in one of the categories listed at the bottom of the form, the baker's choice, such as cakes, pies, etcetera. As the competition is a reality TV production for a television audience, the entrant is to explain to the viewer exactly what the baker is doing and then display the finished product.

Oh, yes, and include a brief introduction of yourself and what winning would mean to you. The baker was to be creative—*all in ten minutes*. A video over ten minutes, even by a second, would be disqualified.

The rules also stated that two original recipes were to be submitted along with the application. Again, this was the baker's choice from any of the categories. All items were to be attached to an email, see address below. Entries received through the U.S. Postal service would be rejected.

Grinning, Tyler slid the pages back over the table to Star. “So, what’s the big deal?”

“A video? Duh?” Her shoulders collapsed. “How am I going to do that?” Her eyes were wide—*how stupid can he be*?

“I can.”

Chapter 11

ENTER THE AMATEUR baking competition? Star was skeptical but Ty's enthusiasm was contagious. He seemed to think he could handle the whole thing from his parent's garage.

A garage? Really?

He insisted he had the equipment in the space over the garage. He said his mom and dad had fixed it up. They did it as an act of encouragement, encouraging him to keep up with his dream of cartoon animation. For awhile anyway—to give it a good shot.

They made a pact with him.

He could live over the garage rent free, mooch off of them for his meals. His mom insisted he do his own laundry, but other than that, he should pursue his dream. They gave him two years once he graduated with a Master's degree from Florida State University, in Tallahassee.

This was his second summer after graduation.

The pact with his parents was about to expire.

"Do you always go this fast?" Star screamed in his ear over the roar of his motorcycle. Clinging to Ty for dear life, her hair escaped the helmet he insisted she wear, strands flying out straight.

"Only when on a caper, Miss Bloom," he yelled back through the wind.

To Star, the only thing missing was Superman's cape. She felt sure they would levitate off the black asphalt of Atlantic Avenue into the clouds, flying like a bird in a straight line from the diner to wherever Superman was taking her.

The shiny black bat-bike swung into a driveway sheltered by arching live oak trees trimmed in an abundance of Spanish moss. Tyler slid off the seat, extended a hand to Star, and engaged the kickstand.

Catching her breath, shoving her hair out of her eyes as she pulled off the helmet, she stood beside the Harley looking at a three car garage, a line of windows above. There was a staircase up the side leading to whatever the space was behind the windows. The house and garage, trimmed in white, were sided with clapboard painted a soft moss green.

Ty caught his breath as well—the sun was dancing on her golden hair.

Star took a step closer to the garage. Nestled next to the stairs was a cozy stone patio. A small glass table, black wrought iron legs, was flanked by two Adirondack chairs painted geranium red. A round table with a red umbrella, matching the color of the chairs, poked up through the center providing shade for sipping iced tea or reading a book.

A predominantly black calico cat sauntered up to Ty, stretched her hind legs, ending with a flick of her toes. She grazed Ty's ankle, performed a figure eight around his feet, then sat next to his sneaker proceeding to comb her fur around her ear with a dainty white paw.

"Meet Cleopatra, Cleo. As you can see she reigns supreme around here." Ty grasped Star's hand pulling her to the stairs. "Come on. I'll show you my studio."

"This is all very nice but I don't see how you can help me in time. The entry has to be received in three days, by midnight."

"Come on Cinderella. I'll show you how."

At the top of the stairs Ty dropped her hand, unlocked the door, opening it wide, motioning to her to enter.

Star stepped into a large open space spanning the three garage bays below. The vaulted ceiling had two skylights per side. The windows on one wall faced the driveway, and on the opposite side faced a secret garden filled with flowers, guarded by towering oaks. The hardwood floors were graced with oriental rugs. A futon, dresser, and lamp table were tucked into one corner at the far end. Ty explained that a small half bath anchored the sleeping area. The opposite corner was composed of a galley kitchen arrangement—studio refrigerator, counter, sink, and microwave oven. A full bath with shower and Jacuzzi was on the other side of the door connecting his studio to the main house.

Other than the small quarters at the end, tables and bookcases lined the walls. Three long tables pushed together held a small printer, a large laser printer, stacks of paper in various colors, two computers, one with three monitors to run his animations.

The computers were connected to a large TV screen mounted on the wall. Star would soon learn that the computers were loaded with the latest in graphic, animation, and sound software. Off to one side sat a large drafting table, then an expanse of cupboard space. Pine paneling covered the walls and ceiling creating a warm atmosphere, a non-intrusive space, a place allowing Tyler to stir his creative juices.

"This is a serious studio, Ty." Star had trailed behind him, eyes wandering, pointing to one thing then another as he explained the equipment and his living area. "What does that panel of buttons control?" Star asked pointing to the side of the door where they had entered.

"One runs shades over the skylights." He pushed the button and dark shades rolled over the glass blocking out the sunlight. "And this one draws the drapes over the front windows. The button next to that takes care of the drapes at the far end. And this one turns on indirect lighting. Keen, huh?"

Star laughed. "Way keen. What business is your dad in? Printing money? This had to cost a fortune."

"My dad, Anthony Jackman, his friends call him Tony, is a computer engineer. And, my mom, Cindy, operates her own real estate agency. As I said, they gave me two years to follow my dream and then I'm on my own. They paid for my college, gave me the Harley as a graduation present along with surprising me with this layout. I can borrow Mom or Dad's car if I have to haul something. Some of the equipment came from the company Dad works for, but the majority was hauled up from his man-cave on the main floor of the house as he upgraded his electronics. He invents stuff. But, he likes this space the best ... I think. That computer setup at the other end of the tables is his. It's kinda fun to work alongside each other. We don't talk, really immersed in what we're doing, but we feel each other's presence."

Star envied the way he talked about his mom and dad. The family was very close it seemed, something she had missed out on. Except for her Gran. "This is really something, but I don't see a camera. How are you going to take the video?"

Tyler hustled to a closet, opened the door. Grinning, he waved at the contents. Three cameras of various sizes, sat on one shelf. Another shelf held numerous lenses. Two tripods leaned against the end wall along with what appeared to be white umbrellas.

"Now, let me show you what I've learned from the Food Network." Noting her raised brows, he replied, "Yeah, I've seen a few shows. After you started cooking at the diner, I wanted to understand more about what you were flipping, mixing up back there. Come on. You have to see your stage."

Grasping her hand, he led her to the door adjoining the main house. It opened onto the second floor hallway, several doors were open off to one side including the bathroom he had mentioned. The hall was cut in the middle with a flowing, curved staircase overlooking an expansive foyer. A cherry wood railing topped white spindles bordering the hall and stairs.

Ty kept hold of her hand slowing his steps so she wouldn't fall as her eyes focused from one viewpoint to another. At the bottom of the stairs, he led her through a dining room and a large family room open to the kitchen.

Waving his arms around, he turned grinning. "Ta Da! Your kitchen awaits, Miss Bloom."

"Oh, Ty, do you mean it? Your mom would let me prepare something in here for the video?"

"Yup. I haven't asked her yet. You know I just had the idea when I picked you up. I couldn't exactly call when we were on the bike."

"Thank God for that. I was already scared and if you had taken your hands off the handle bars, well ..." Her words trailed off as she walked behind the counter in the middle of the kitchen. There was a gas stovetop with counter space on each side, granite counters over honey-pine cabinets. Twirling around she took in the layout, already envisioning herself—the refrigerator on one end, along with a sink, and then double ovens were all within a step or two of the stovetop.

"Ty, can you capture the warmth of this kitchen in the video? It will be such a wonderful backdrop. Oh, but I need a mixer, pots, sauté pans, or maybe not. I have no idea yet what I'll want to cook up in the video."

"Yes, Cinderella, all right here." Tyler pushed open the small sliding doors along the wall at the back of one of the counters displaying a mixer, blender, food processer—one large, one small for chopping nuts. "Now, let's go back to my studio and workup a game plan."

"You'd better call your mom first. She may not want me to invade her kitchen."

Chapter 12

THE BLACK HARLEY sped down Atlantic Avenue from Ormond Beach. Ty let up on the gas feeling Star's arms circling his waist, clutching him tightly. Neither screamed questions above the roar—Ty planning the kitchen setup for filming tomorrow, Star doubting the whole competition thing.

A video?

A very iffy proposition.

She trusted Ty, but this wasn't one of his sketches, wasn't a cartoon. This was real life, her life. She'd read about the camera's eye—loving some people, rejecting others, ending careers before they even started. What if they, whoever they were, didn't accept her into the baking competition? Then what?

Parking behind the diner, Ty chained the Harley to the bike stand. Star leaned against his arm, spoke in a hushed voice. "Let's keep the competition a secret. If by some wild chance I'm accepted, then I'll have to tell Charlie ... Wanda ... rearrange my schedule. I have to be careful, Ty. I can't jeopardize my job."

"Don't worry. I won't say a word. We both have tomorrow off ... no problem," he said leaning closer, whispering, "This is but the first step to making your dreams come true, Miss Bloom."

Shaking her head, back to reality, clearing the dream away, she hustled to take her post behind the grill.

The shift was a foggy blur—flipping burgers, mixing batch after batch of meatball mini-tarts that Tyler served with dollops of spicy cranberry glaze. The tartlets had become a big seller especially with moms finding something their kids liked to eat. How great was that?

Star spastically jotted notes on a small pad, tearing off the page, stuffing the page in her pocket, a pocket full outlining what to do, to say—a script for tomorrow. She and Ty kept whispering, adding, discarding, swapping dialog, preparing for the video shoot.

Finishing their shift, Tyler offered to take her home on his Harley promising to slow the bat-bike a notch. Ah ha, he had nudged ahead of Ash.

Before going to bed, her mind a jumble of opportunities for the video Ty laid out before her, Star sat on her blow-up mattress, leaned against the wall, and called Gran.

Gran barely said hello before Star began rattling off news of a baking competition—prize of fifty grand for the winner, a video required for entry, Tyler to produce the video, shooting the video tomorrow because it had to be emailed the next day before midnight.

When Star paused to breathe, Gran cut in, asking Star to repeat what she just said, slower. Then she made her granddaughter promise to call when she was accepted into the competition.

No *if*. When!

"I told you, Star, that your love for baking would someday be revealed as your path in life, and here it is. Don't forget to call."

"I won't forget, Gran. I love you."

"Love you too, sweetie."

Chapter 13

TY PICKED HER UP at six o'clock sharp.

Today was their day off.

Today was video production day.

The shops along Atlantic Avenue whizzed by the car window as Star shielded her eyes from the glare of the early morning sun. Tyler had borrowed his mom's white Lincoln Navigator, big enough to haul around her real estate clients, or props and supplies for her son's cartoon endeavors.

Leaning back against the headrest, Star blew out a breath. She wondered what Ty thought about her studio apartment when he had picked her up. Glancing around when he stepped inside to help carry the boxes, she saw him take note of the green leatherette beanbag near the patio door, the little round bistro table she bought for five bucks at a consignment shop, and the blow-up-mattress covered with a bright blue blanket sprinkled with daisies. Her studio was a far cry from his studio. The word studio certainly had different meanings depending on how you looked at it—his studio, then her studio, a tiny room in comparison, a very cheap rental.

Star's heart frozen in fear one minute, thumped against her ribs the next in anticipation that something wonderful was going to happen today. Closing her eyes, hunching her shoulders, the video loomed in her mind—a chance, maybe the only chance to break out of her downward spiral. It was now or never.

If she didn't get into the competition, then she'd take it as a sign—having her own bakery was a pipedream.

On the other hand, Ty could hardly contain his excitement. He had tossed and turned most of the night producing the video in his head, swapping one clip with another. "I bet your grandmother liked your idea of featuring her taffy." Ty didn't speed this morning, rounded the corners carefully so the supplies and equipment Star had packed for the filming didn't fall over on the bags of ingredients tucked on the floor behind his seat. He was trying to help her relax but he could see he was not succeeding.

Letting his mind wander as he drove, Ty visualized his mother giving instructions to the cleaning lady—the kitchen was to be spotless. He smiled, thinking of how excited she was when he had filled her in on his plans for a video, providing, of course, that she gave the okay to use her kitchen.

Excited? She had been overjoyed. Partly because her son was actually going to produce something, and partly out of curiosity to meet the young woman Tyler was bringing to the house. It was a first and she didn't care if he insisted it was only a job.

Tyler's lips twitched, turning up ever so slightly, remembering when he told his dad about the video, and his dad deciding he'd stay at the house, have an extra cup of coffee before going into work. Ty knew his dad was just as excited about meeting Star as his mother.

"What? What did you say?"

"Gran did agree with my choice of featuring her taffy in the video," Star said. "She thought it was a wonderful idea and agreed the taffy recipe could wow them. And, the taffy would give me a good story to tell when I introduce myself in the video. Humanize me, she said."

Suddenly she felt she was asking way too much of her friend. Glancing at him, so intent on his driving. What was he thinking? Second thoughts?

"Ty, are you sure you want to do this? I can't pay you, but I will repay you some day no matter—"

"Hey, I'm not asking you to pay me. Who knows, maybe I'll enter this video in a competition of my own. A comedy about making taffy—"

"Comedy? That's not funny. Do you think your parents are going to laugh at me?"

"No way. Relax. Mom and Dad are looking forward to meeting the next bakery queen." Reaching across the console, he patted her hand. Her skin was as smooth as he had imagined it to be. He liked the way she fixed her hair this morning. The soft waves falling around her shoulders were going to look great. He knew the camera was going to have a love affair with her. Maybe someday, maybe after she wins, he'll give her a celebratory kiss.

He had dated a few girls at Florida State, nothing serious. Girls thought he was some kind of geek. They laughed at his cartoons but didn't appreciate the artistic side like Star did. Star was different.

Parking in the driveway, they hopped out of the car as his mom and dad rushed out of the house to help. Tyler knew they were dying to meet the girl he was bringing home. It didn't matter to them that he was just helping her out.

His mom held out her hand. "It's so nice to meet you. The kitchen is spic and span for your video."

"Mrs. Jackman, I hope you didn't go to a lot of trouble, really your kitchen is—"

Laughing, she said, "Please, call me Cindy—"

"And I'm Tony, Tyler's dad. We're so happy to meet you and wish you success in the competition. Now, let Cindy and I lend a hand ... my goodness. All this? Are you cooking up a feast?"

"No, not a feast but I hope you like my Gran's taffy ... Atlantic City Salt Water Taffy. Her world famous recipe ... well, maybe not world famous ..."

"Hey, after you two finish with the video, and you win, your Gran's taffy *will* be world famous."

"Okay, everybody. Let's get these bags inside so Star and I can get started. And, no audience allowed. You'll get a private showing tonight." Tyler grinned as he handed two sacks to his mom, then a carton to his dad. *Oh, this is going to be fun. Star looks nervous. Nothing like a little dose of stage fright to bring out the best in an actress.*

Chapter 14

THE STAGE WAS SET!

Star dressed in a white, short-sleeved cotton blouse with a black skirt hitting just above her knees. It was the same outfit that she wore at the diner when she was hired as a waitress. Waves of blonde hair swept her shoulders and white low-cut sneakers put a spring in her step. She'd tied a plain white square of cotton around her waist.

Ty fussed with the white umbrellas until the soft diffused lighting suited him. Turning to the equipment, he attached a special zoom lens to each of two Nikon cameras, steadied in place on tripods. A handle to the side of the tripod base allowed him to turn freely from refrigerator, to sink, to Star—the focal point. Every angle would be captured on the memory chips of the two cameras.

The director made a small exception to his *no audience* edict. He allowed Cleopatra to enter the kitchen. She perched on a counter to the side, slightly behind Tyler, the only piece of counter she was allowed on. She sat very still, purring, her white front paws occasionally kneading the flecked black granite, and baring her teeth with a wide yawn when there was a break in the action. At times, a flash of fur could be seen—a quick dart to her food dish, water bowl, out the cat door for relief, returning with a mighty leap to her perch. Superman would have been proud.

First, Tyler was going to film a short clip testing the sound quality, the lighting, and to let Star settle comfortably into her role. Tapping the camera button, he pointed at Star to begin.

"My name is Star Bloom, originally from Hoboken, New Jersey, and now Daytona Beach, Florida. Today, I'm—"

"Cut. Come see."

Heads together, they looked at the test clip.

"The lighting's good, Ty, and—"

"A deer caught in the headlights," Ty mumbled. Glancing around the kitchen, he spotted a folding chair, stuck it in front of the tripod of the center camera. He positioned a kitchen chair to the side of the second camera. This camera would run continuously, to capture angles, shots to splice in where needed when editing.

Loping around the kitchen, opening, closing cabinets, Tyler tucked a cereal box, a five-pound package of flour, a package of sugar off the same shelf under his arms, grabbed a package of egg noodles holding it between his knees, and a pack of chocolate candy kisses under his chin.

Shuffling to the kitchen chair, he lined up the flour, cereal, and sugar. Then to the folding chair he propped the chocolate kisses up against the noodles.

Star returned to her position behind the cook top. What was the director doing? Cleo, also mesmerized by his actions, snapped her head following each move.

Tyler made another adjustment, moving the tripod back a couple of inches to be sure he included the bottom edge of the gas burner when Star heated the corn syrup, butter, and water. He nudged the marble slab where Star would pour the mixture to cool slightly before performing the final acts—separating the batch, adding color and flavor, cutting into pieces, wrapping in wax paper, twisting the ends of paper to seal the candy. He knew it would take her way more than ten minutes for the introduction and to make the taffy—the do or die rules of the competition. He'd deal with that issue later.

Fun, fun, fun.

"Okay. Star. Talk to Benny." Ty pointed to the egg noodles and kisses on the stool, "and the Butterworth sisters on the chair. Explain to them how to make taffy."

"Ty, you crazy director." She rushed to give him a hug, darted back ready to begin again.

"Hello, My name is Star Bloom. I grew up near Atlantic City, and as a kid, my grandmother and I made Salt Water Taffy. I tagged along, carrying the basket of candy, as Gran sold it to vendors along the beach. Today I'm going to share with you the fun of creating her red and white striped peppermint taffy."

Star took a deep breath, her mind going blank. She couldn't remember what she was going to say next. Tyler clicked off the camera, rocked back on his heels beaming. Not responding to her sudden lack of memory, he hustled around the island, pulling her behind the camera.

"Take a look at this. You're fabulous," he said, running the brief segment.

"It does look okay, I guess."

"You guess? It's wonderful."

"I'm talking too fast."

"No, no, no. It's fine. You have a lot to tell Benny. Don't forget, say everything you want to get out because I'll edit it down. You have your talking points?"

"Yes. Intro, put ingredients in the pan, heat, talk, pour onto marble slab to cool. Switch to divided portions, add color, roll, pull. End ... oh I don't remember how to sign off."

"This is Star Bloom from Atlantic City. Say that because you will cement who you are and the name of your candy and Atlantic City. Okay, now, back to your position. Keep breathing. Don't forget to talk to Benny and the Butterworth sisters. You're doing great."

• • •

TY TURNED OFF the camera as Star slid down the refrigerator door to the floor at the same time his mother walked in. Thinking Star had fainted she rushed to her side, kneeling on the floor. "Star, are you all right? Ty, hand me that bottle of water by Cleo."

Ty grabbed his bottle, handed the other to his mom and slid down the refrigerator beside Star.

"Hey, you two, what's going on?"

Both smiled. Tension, adrenalin spent. "We just wrapped up, Mom. Wait 'til you see. When's Dad coming home?"

"An hour, give or take. He's picking up a pizza for the show."

"What show, Mrs. Jackman?"

"Hey, it's Cindy, remember?" she said laughing. "Your show. And, I'll tell you, we can be very critical. Having lived with Tyler's cartoons, we learned to stop telling him everything was great. We're supportive, but if it's terrible, or we didn't understand, we told him. Didn't we, dear?"

"You sure did. Okay, Star, up and at 'em. We have an hour for the first editing session. Bring your water."

"How about some iced tea ... a little caffeine will perk you up," Cindy said. "You go ahead. I'll bring a tray up."

Chapter 15

TYLER AND STAR sipped the last drop of iced tea as Star Bloom from Atlantic City signed off—*Invite your friends and their kids over for a Taffy pull*—the screen fading to black.

"Okay, Miss Bloom, let's go meet our critics over a slice of pizza and a glass of Dad's best merlot."

"Ty, you did a masterful job, made me look good, but I'm not sure my words are right."

"As I said, let's go see what our public thinks."

"Can we go to the kitchen first? I left a mess for your mom."

Ty just grinned. If he knew his mother, the kitchen was already slick as a whistle, but he tagged along, walked close.

"Oh no. Everything's picked up. I should have done it while you were editing."

"Come on worrywart, the theatre is ready."

"Theatre?"

"Come, Miss Bloom. Your public awaits."

"Did you bring the files?"

"Hey, Miss Bloom, my dad's an engineer. A wide-screen TV is connected to my computer, just like the TV screen on my studio wall."

"About time you two came down," Tony said.

"You didn't peek did you, Dad?"

"Never. Now help yourself to pizza. Cindy will pour the wine, then crank her up, son."

Star couldn't eat, not until the verdict was in, but a little wine might help settle her nerves. Thanking Cindy, Star took a seat in the third row of soft, black leather chairs. Ty set a plate with two pieces of pizza on his lap. Whispering, he raised his glass to hers. "Cheers."

Ty still had to cut thirty seconds but he wanted to wait for their reaction, and suggestions, on where to cut.

After a bite of pizza, he leaned forward, tapped his dad's shoulder. "Roll it."

The screen snapped to life filled with Star smiling out at them.

"Hello, my name is Star Bloom."

Star couldn't watch, walked to the back of the room and faced the wall, wine glass in hand listening to herself. When she heard the sign-off words silence filled the room. *They didn't like it. I was awful. How stupid, presumptuous—"*

"Bravo, bravo," Tony and Cindy sang out in unison. "Star ... where ... come here, girl," Tony said.

"You're terrific, sweetheart," Cindy added looking around for the young woman.

Tyler continued to sit in the big leather chair, elbows on his knees, enjoying the moment. His mom was right. Star was terrific.

Star was afraid to move. Did they mean it? A tear ran down her cheek, just one before Cindy and Tony were by her side, hugging her.

Then everyone settled back in their seats, Tony and Cindy swiveling around to face Tyler.

"Where can I cut thirty seconds? Suggestions?" Tyler asked.

Cindy and Tony looked at each other and shrugged. They didn't want to cut any of it. Between them they came up with a few seconds where Star wasn't talking, stirring the sugar in the pan, pulling the taffy.

• • •

TYLER THOUGHT FOR SURE their edits would do it plus a couple of his own. Eager to try, he and Star scampered to his studio to make the changes.

Within an hour Tyler had made the final edits. He was ready to put all the pieces together to complete Star's application. Star retrieved the flash drive from her purse with the application form she had worked on until one in the morning. There were boxes requesting why she was entering the competition, her baking experience, and what it would mean to her if she won.

Tyler pulled up the Amateur Baker Competition website, clicked on the button labeled: To Enter Click Here.

Heads inches apart, eyes fixed on the screen, Tyler began filling in the information from the printout of the form Star had prepared. The initial boxes were straight forward—first name, last name, address. Telephone number.

Next were browse buttons to upload the video file, prepared application form, and the photo ID that Star scanned into a file. The files uploaded, the only thing left was the payment method of the $200 entry fee. The entry fee was refundable if the baker was not selected for the competition. Star handed Ty her credit card. He selected the Master Card from a drop-down menu and typed in the card numbers, and expiration date.

Ty looked at Star, his mouse hovering over the ENTER button.

She couldn't conceive of any circumstance where she would pull out. Come hell or high water, sickness or a broken leg, she would compete.

"Are you ready? Everything okay with you?" he asked. "Should I hit ENTER?"

"Hit it." Star wondered how the video and her application would be received. So much riding on it. Her life would not end. But her dream might.

• • •

TONY HAD PACKED UP the car ready for Tyler to drive Star home. Thanking Ty's parents over and over for their help, Star exchanged another round of hugs. Tyler held the car door open for her and then slid behind the wheel.

With a wave, they were on the road.

It was almost midnight when Tyler parked the car, transferred the boxes back to her studio that they had carted to the car that morning.

Saying goodnight on the doorstep, Ty wrapped her in his arms telling her that she was wonderful. She kissed his cheek and disappeared behind the closed door.

Her lids heavy, body drained, she hit the blowup mattress without undressing, dreaming of Benny and the Butterworth sisters savoring red and white striped peppermint taffy.

Chapter 16

MANNY AND ELIZABETH had been married for almost two years and he had never seen this expression on her face. His wife stood facing him, grinning from ear to ear. She didn't say a word, just stood there grinning. Even their two dogs, Peaches and Maggie, flanking her side were grinning along with their mistress. Manny tilted his head at the canines. Something was up.

No hint from how his wife was dressed. When they were on assignment both dressed in all black, head to toe. But at home, Liz was a delightful rainbow of color—lemon, lime, plum, and cherry red. Today, a light turquoise T-shirt floated over kiwi shorts, her toes a mango-orange.

"Okay, I give up. What happened? You're smiling so I doubt you wrecked the car. Our dogs can't have puppies. Did you buy the winning ticket to the state lottery?"

"Better than all of that, Manny, my dear husband."

"Well ... the lottery—"

"We're going to have a baby!"

Manny's eyes began to bulge, a grin slowly creeping across his face. He was going to be a father. At forty-two, he was finally going to be a father. He stepped to the love of his life, wrapping her in his arms, their eyes misting, familiar bodies folding together in a tender embrace.

"Calls for champagne," he whispered into her ear, ringlets of red hair swirling around his lips. "But... you can't drink ... so, neither will I."

"How about a glass of grape juice?" Liz giggled as the telephone rang.

Manny kissed her sweet puckered mouth as she reached for his cell clipped to his belt and held it to his ear.

Without looking at the caller ID, he answered. "Salinas."

"Manny. Alex Donovan here. Did I get you at a bad time?"

"Depends on how you look at it, Alex. You interrupted one of the best moments of my life. Liz, rather my precious wife Stitch as I like to call her, just told me I'm going to be a father."

"Hey, congratulations. When's the baby due?"

Liz, her ear next to Manny's, whispered, "December."

"In case you didn't hear, Alex, that would be December. Now tell me why you're calling so Stitch and I can get on celebrating with popcorn and grape juice."

"Umm, grape juice. You're a good man, Salinas."

Manny released his grip on his wife and flopped onto the couch grinning at her. Her body aglow, a perpetual grin on her face, Liz bobbed her head up and down, mouthing she would go pop the corn.

"Okay, Alex, give. You never call just to say hello."

"My agents have been picking up chatter. It escalated in the last few weeks. I need someone local, someone who knows the people, knows how to ferret out what's going on. I thought of you. Can you check around for me? On the clock, of course."

"Sure. What kind of chatter? I thought the bad guys were too smart to *chatter* these days."

"Yeah, they are. But we've intercepted coded messages of several different kinds, even Twitter of all places, and someone called in with a tip. Wouldn't give his name."

"Okay ... so what's it about?"

"Fireworks. BIG fireworks. Several targets, simultaneously, in Florida."

Manny leaned forward, his gaze turning to the kitchen door. A sudden grip of tension in his belly. He was awash with love for his adorable wife. Nothing would ever happen to her as long as he was alive. "Where specifically in Florida, and when?"

"All over—Miami, Orlando. Disney's there you know. The families, kids—that place would give a very visible bang for the buck. Cape Canaveral—Kennedy Space Center. NASCAR came up—Daytona Beach."

"When?"

"We don't know exactly. Nothing definitive."

"Names?" Manny's fingers ran over his moustache.

"Nothing yet. We're scanning passports, likely destinations, cities with incoming flights—Atlanta, Orlando, Miami. Of course, they could come across our southern border or northern border for that matter. The nine-eleveners traveled from Canada."

"May be here already."

"Could be, but the chatter doesn't indicate that. Seems more like the planning stage, planning to congregate here."

"I'll check around. See what I can turn up." Manny sighed.

"Thanks, Manny. And congratulations again. My best to Elizabeth."

Chapter 17

PEERING OVER THE TOP of her spectacles, Jane's eyes flicked from side to side. "Lizzy, there's a parking spot. Over there. Last one. Looks like business is picking up."

"Sure does—too late for breakfast and early for lunch. I wonder what happened."

"Come on, dear. Star said she'd save us a booth. I thought she was kidding."

Liz, a beam of sunshine in a lemon T over orange capris and sandals, took hold of her aunt's elbow. Stepping sprightly from the car, the little diner beckoned them in, tube lighting rocking with the well fed jukebox.

They waved at Star behind the order window as Tyler came rushing up to them.

"Come with me, mademoiselles," he said grinning. "Your table is waiting."

Sliding in on either side of the booth, they looked up wondering what Tyler would do next. They both got a kick out of him, and he never disappointed.

Tyler pulled two menus from around his back placing them on the table with a flourish and slight bow. "Your menus. Hot off the press ... well a week ago. Jane, you were spot on the money. I drew up a new menu featuring Star's meatball mini-tarts punctuated with my cartoons. Charlie and Wanda said to give it a try and just look what happened. Business exploded. It's been crazy like this for a few days. Catch the kids menu at the bottom."

"Tyler, the menu looks wonderful. Fun." Liz said. "And from the looks of the kids in here ... what are they doing over there?" Liz pointed to a table against the wall.

"Star's idea. I ran off some of the cartoons for the kids to color on the back of the paper placemats. See." With a slight of hand, Tyler flipped over the placemat. "Would you like a cup or two of crayons? I'm sure there's a purple to match your dress, Jane ... including the roses. See the little corner labeled, *A Happy Diner*. It's you ... bouffant and all." Tyler stood beaming as two little girls from the booth behind Liz erupted in the giggles. Tyler leaned close, whispered, "The kids took to it, so Wanda ordered a few hundred from the printer."

Standing up straight, he pushed his glasses up on his nose. "Star will join you in a couple of minutes. Charlie's taking over the grill so she can join you for a cup of coffee. She's happy you accepted her invitation. She wanted you to see the menu. Have to run. Oh, Jane. Hot chocolate, whipped cream, and chocolate sprinkles?"

"You devil, you remembered." Winking at Tyler, Jane's pink lips spread into a flirty smile.

"Remembered? Take another look at your cartoon... you have to color the roses red, and a little chocolate brown crayon on those sprinkles don't you think?"

Tyler hustled off as Star passed him, reminding him of their secret not to tell about the video. First hugging Jane, she slid in next to Liz.

"So, how do you like the new menus? Ty's drawings?"

"Wonderful, dear. And the idea of crayons for the children trying to match the cartoons on the walls is very clever. I take it the owners are happy?"

"Yeah. They were a little skeptical at first, but it seemed to bolster the idea of a happy diner. Ty's working up a cartoon of the Wurlitzer, little musical notes whirling around the jukebox. Something we didn't expect, a couple of the regulars recognized the initials under the drawings, TJ, as Tyler's. They began asking for his autograph. That's when Charlie made a deal with a printer friend for copies of just the cartoons. Naturally all were topped with a caricature of the diner for the kids to color. They love the late model cars parked in front. Then the adult guests, especially the tourists, also began asking Tyler to autograph them."

Tyler returned with the coffees and hot chocolate, beaming again through his horn-rimmed glasses.

"Tyler, the drawings are wonderful but you must include a cartoon of yourself. Your guests would love it, signed by their favorite server, don't you think?" Aunt Jane looked up at Tyler over her wire rimmed glasses.

"Capital idea, Jane." He looked over his glasses, mimicking her look, then dashed off with a little girl tugging his hand, dragging him to her parents, asking for a cartoon of the meatball tart wearing a bow tie and polka dot shirt.

Jane laughed.

Liz looked wistfully at the little girl. "Adorable."

"Lizzy, tell Star your big news."

Star turned to Liz, her blue eyes big, questioning.

"Manny and I are having a baby."

"Oh, Liz, hugs for you," Star squealed, wrapping her arms around Liz. "Congratulations. When?"

"Not until December."

"How did Manny take the news?"

"He's ecstatic," Jane blurted out, smiling ear to ear.

"Which reminds me, Manny and I have an appointment. I'm sorry, but I think we have to bring this little coffee klatch to an end," Liz said with a frowny face.

Star returned the frowny face. "If you must. I'll walk out with you."

Leaving the Wurly music arm in arm out into the humid air, Star saw Ash walking up the driveway.

"Ash, hi. Come here, I want you to meet my two best friends, Jane and Liz. They stopped by for coffee. And you two, meet my friend Ash."

Ash shook Jane's hand fluttering in front of him. "Nice to meet you, Jane and Liz. I can see by the smile on your faces you enjoyed the new atmosphere ... the cartoons."

"The menus were Jane's idea," Star said squeezing her aunt's arm.

"Oh, it was nothing. We'll be back soon. Won't we, Lizzy?"

"Absolutely. I feel we had a hand in adding a little spice to those meatball tarts. Nice to meet you, Ash."

Star hugged them, waved goodbye, and turned to Ash. "Coffee?"

"No, I'm off on an assignment. I stopped by to let you know I'll walk you home tonight."

"Great. You know where to find me. I like your reporter clothes. Tan trousers, white polo shirt—casual, put the people you interview for your stories at ease, and—"

"I missed you last night." He reached over, his thumb grazing her cheek. "A speck of flour."

She smiled at the gesture, hoping it was more than a speck of flour. "I missed you too. I had stuff I had to do last night."

Shifting his gaze to the side then back. "Okay. Tonight. Closing. Still nine o'clock?"

Star nodded, watched him return to his car. She didn't trust her voice. *Tongue-tied? Come on, you're acting like a school girl, missy.*

Chapter 18

THE BLISSFUL IMAGE of Liz having a baby flitted in and out of Star's mind as she prepared another late lunch order of meatball mini-tarts for a mother with three lively toddlers. The mother, looking at her waiter, whispered that the tarts were a conspiracy to keep her children contained. She came to the diner for the menus and a cup of crayons, everything else, as far as she was concerned, was gravy. Except for a cup of coffee and a side order of blueberry pie, if you please.

During the shift, Star felt Ty looking at her. If she looked up, his brows would arch, questioning? Had she heard from the bakeoff competition—was she in?

Star just shook her head. She wasn't sure if it was nerves or just a very humid day—her visor's sweatband was wicking in overdrive. She kept checking her cell phone—had she turned it off, were the batteries dead? No ... she wasn't selected and they were skipping a call, sending a rejection by snail mail. *Don't be absurd,* she thought snatching an order slip from the wire above the grill.

Ty's eyes were constantly locking on her until she finally gave him the look—*stop it!*

Retrieving another can of whole-berry cranberry sauce from the shelf, she felt her cell phone vibrate in her apron pocket. Fumbling for the phone, knocking a spatula to the floor, her hand grazing a splash of olive oil, she turned her back to the grill holding the phone to her ear with sticky fingers.

Ty saw her turn, cell in her hand.

He watched. Was this it?

Star didn't budge a whisker. He could tell she wasn't breathing—it had to be the call they were waiting for. It must be good news. Bad news doesn't take this long?

Suddenly, Star twirled, her eyes darting around the diner to find him. He was at the third booth, holding a pot of coffee mid-air. Star started jumping up and down, fists in the air as she raced from the grill. Ty quickly moved the coffee pot to safety on the booth's table startling the guests. At the same exact moment, the cook threw her arms around their waiter.

Without saying a word, both grinning, Star, with a slight skip in the air, returned to the grill and Ty topped off booth number three's coffee.

Finally, there was a lull in the diner. Orders were filled, and no one was coming in the door. The Wurlitzer rocked out a Kelly Clarkson ballad as Ty strode to Star's side. "So, when? Where?"

"The coordinator, that's what she called herself, said the producer rented a building. Set up a television studio in Daytona Beach."

"Where?"

"On Williamson Boulevard—off International Speedway. She's emailing all the information. The call was to let me know I'm in. Ty, I AM IN! Oh my God, I have to tell Wanda ... Charlie. They're going to have a fit."

"What's going on here?" Charlie asked stepping up to the grill ready to relieve Star for her break.

Inhaling a deep breath, Star quickly told him what she and Ty had been up to, adding how it started with her friend's visit. "My friend Jane, you know ... bouffant pink hair—"

"Yes, I know the cartoon."

"Well, Jane suggested I enter a baking competition, Ty made a video of me for the Florida Amateur Baker Competition, that's what it's called. The competition coordinator just notified me ...

I'm in ... Monday, in seven days." Star paused, gasped for air, plunging on. "Can you give me the time off? Please, please, say yes."

Star saw Ty's lips move. "Monday?"

Charlie caught Wanda out of the corner of his eye coming out of the office to see what the commotion was about. "Give you time off for what?" Wanda asked.

Charlie, his face pinched replied, "Seems our cook entered some kind of a cooking contest. What're we going to do now?"

"We're going to wish her well." Wanda moved to give Star a hug. "When I have a minute, you have to tell me about this contest."

Charlie was a little more pragmatic.

Looking at the grill that would once again be his responsibility, he had a slight smile on his face. "Okay, okay. If Wanda says *no problem*, then *there's no problem*. Just remember, if you make it to the finals, you said you'd stay the summer."

• • •

THE COMPETITION RULES landed in Star's email inbox within seconds after she received the call notifying her that she was selected to participate. Ty waited as she scanned the message on her phone's display. She quickly whispered each point. "Oh my God, Ty, there will be one round the first day. Maybe two rounds the next day ... unless I'm eliminated. Every episode ... Ty, episodes like a real TV series. Every episode, except the first will feature one or two rounds, maybe three."

Star looked up at the pot rack, closed her eyes, gulped a big breath and continued. "The baking category, such as cakes, cookies, pies, will be divulged at the beginning of each round—not before. Bring your personal best recipes. You will also be given mystery recipes to display your baking knowledge, skill. There will be a minimum of seven rounds. Must arrive at the studio, directions to follow, by 6:30 a.m. sharp. If you are traveling, make arrangements to stay for the duration of the competition—until you are sent home. The winner will be awarded $50,000."

Star grinned at Ty. There it was again—$50,000. It wasn't a typo.

• • •

"GRAN, I'M IN."

"Sweetheart, that's wonderful. When does it start?"

"Next Monday. Can you send me a few of your favorite recipes—tried and true? I have several of yours, plus the ones we talked about, but I want to be armed with more. I'm not sure how it's all going to work, equipment, stove, oven ... but I'll call you when I find out."

"How about if I send you my little cookbook, the metal one, three-hole punched pages. I always typed my favorites on my old Smith-Corona. Some I wrote with a pen. Many have my notes in the margin. Do you remember it, dear? Six by eight inches, silver metal? Remember?"

"Oh, Gran, of course I remember. Some of the pages, the banana nut bread, have flour stuck to them." Star smiled as she spoke, wiping away a tear. "How are you, Gran? Everything okay? Taking your heart medication?"

"I'm fine dear. I'll get my recipe book in the mail today ... oh, post office is about to close. No, I'll call FedEx right now You'll have it tomorrow afternoon. Now, you keep me posted ... every step of the way, young lady."

"I will, Gran. Love you."

"Love you too, dear."

Chapter 19

THE COMPETITION

MONDAY

THE WHITE LINCOLN cruised down International Speedway, the sun cresting the horizon, rays bouncing off the rearview mirror hitting Tyler in the eyes. Squinting, he turned left onto Williamson Boulevard, and soon turned left again into the driveway and parking lot of a mid-size cement block building. A large, unmarked, white semi truck was parked at the back of the lot. More than twelve cars were parked along the side of the lot shaded by a line of trees. An older woman, white slacks, pink T-shirt, was locking the door of a small blue car marred by a crease stretching across the back fender.

Ty glanced over at Star, her eyes riveted out the windshield. She was nervous.

Way more than nerves. Star tried to breathe in rhythm hoping a steady flow of air into her lungs would tamp down the nerves, release the tension.

What was wrong with her? She was a pastry chef. She'd landed a job at a five-star hotel restaurant. Didn't she?

This was no big deal.

Oh yeah? She was kidding herself. What was at stake? Only her future, her life.

"It's okay, you know," Ty said punctuating each word. "You *are* going to be okay."

Star hitched the strap of the backpack up on her shoulder, picked up the red tote between her feet on the floor mat, and flashed a smile at Ty. "Wish me luck," she said sliding out of the car into the sunshine, humid air smacking her in the face.

"Good luck and I'll be here to pick you up. Give me a call, or text if you'll be later than six, otherwise I'll be here."

"Okay. Thanks." Smoothing her black slacks, straightening the collar of her white blouse, the same outfit she wore in the video with the exception of changing a skirt to a pair of slacks, she was ready.

Setting her backpack straight, chin up, Star marched through the door into a new world of bright lights, cameras on rolling sleds, and the buzz of anticipation that something big was about to take place.

Wide-eyed, gaping at the scene before her, she was caught by surprise at the elaborate set up of a television studio. The producers obviously meant business—the filming of a TV reality show, a show of amateur bakers, contestants vying for a chance to transform their everyday existence into a dream of becoming recognized as a professional baker. In Star's case, compete for the prize money, money that would make it possible to open a little bakery, publish a cookbook, a wildly successful cookbook.

Holding that image in her mind, she strode to the contestant's work area.

The producers had put together a very charming, colorful but tasteful environment for the competition, an area that would soon showcase the drama of a baking competition.

She smiled at the individual baker's setup, almost identical to Cindy's kitchen except now there were five rows, two stations per row, separated by a center aisle. Each station was like a galley kitchen, delineated by butcher-block counters, front and back.

Standing between the counters, the bakers had access to the stovetop in the middle of the front counter, or the ovens behind, as well as cabinets filled with prepositioned supplies such as flour and sugar, baking pans and utensils.

The space was open, counter to ceiling, so the bakers could see the host at the front, and each other at all times.

Off to one side of each station was a bright red refrigerator—one refrigerator shared by two bakers. Matching red mixer, blender, striped hand towels, oven mitts, were lined up on the counters. Star chuckled. Her visor was the same red as the refrigerator and appliances. She chose the color hoping it would bring her luck and easy to spot her. "Recognition is key," Tyler had said. Plus he wanted her to stand out in more ways than being the cutest baker in the competition.

The cement-block walls sported a fresh coat of white paint on three sides. The fourth side consisted of a bank of picture windows framing a lush woodsy landscape of oak and pine trees towering over flowering bushes with red, orange, and yellows blooms. A serene scene compared to the drumming of hearts beating in the chests of the anxious bakers. Inside, faux trees had been strategically placed to soften the room of the one-time electronics factory.

Thankfully, the air conditioning was working.

A wide area, a stage, fronted the baker's stations with a doorway opening to the back to what Star presumed were once offices.

Spotting her name on the counter, left side, second row, she strode toward her station introducing herself to another contestant checking out her space, and then to a young man setting up behind her. They would share the red refrigerator. Checking the cabinets lining her work station, Star found everything she needed, all provided by the producers at no charge to the contestants, except for the entry fee.

A bald man, official looking in a suit and tie, hustled up to Star, introduced himself as Jim Whisk, one of the two producers, explaining he would be acting as the show's host. He didn't stop to chat, hustling off to each of the other nine bakers.

Striding to his place at the front of the hall, Whisk picked up a cordless microphone lying on a side table. He turned to face the eager, nervous smiles of the ten wanna-be bakers all dressed in their street clothes–slacks with colorful T-shirts—stripes, flowered, or solid. Slacks were plain, but of multiple colors.

It was show time.

"Welcome, everyone, to the Florida Amateur Baker Competition. Relax, I'll let you know when we begin filming the show. First, let me introduce my co-producer, Stephanie Hall."

An attractive thirty-something blonde woman, dressed in black slacks under a long-sleeve white silk shirt, a gold chain draped around her slender neck, gold hoops at her ears, looked smart and professional strutting up in high heels to the host. She stood beside Jim, smiled and nodded to the group arrayed before her. Ms. Hall towered over her co-producer by a foot. When Mr. Whisk turned his head to welcome his co-producer, he revealed a sandy-haired ponytail neatly held back by an elastic band.

Hearing a stifled whistle for Stephanie Hall, Star glanced around at the two cameramen leaning back, relaxing, waiting for the show to begin, waiting to start maneuvering the camera sleds, zooming in and out of the action.

"Okay, Steph, are we ready to film the first episode?"

"Absolutely. Take it away, Jim."

Star and the other contestants stood like soldiers at their battle stations, the two cameramen sat forward, eyes peeled through the lens at the host.

"Hello, and welcome to the first Florida Amateur Baker Competition. There's a lot at stake, folks—publication of a cookbook, guest appearances on various television shows. Oh, and did I mention a grand prize ... $50,000 to the winner of this season's show?"

Laughter erupted from the ten bakers, clapping at his pronouncement of the grand prize.

"With each episode you will be tested on your ability to bake something tasty, as close to perfection as you can get, all under extreme pressure. At the end of each episode, one of you will be named Star Baker for that day's category ... for example Star Pie Baker. And, one will be eliminated. At the end of the final episode, end of the series, there will be one winner.

"Our contestants are from all walks of life—a lawyer, a fireman, a stay-at-home dad, a housewife ready to cut loose now that her kids are off to college, a short-order cook, to mention a few. With every episode you will work your magic in three different segments, but within the same category. Today, we begin with pies, pies, and more pies. The first pie segment will be one you lay your claim to fame on, your personal best, the one you've baked a hundred times, the pie called for by family and friends."

With his words, Star visualized the email she'd received from the producers listing the categories—cakes, cookies, pies and tarts, breads, desserts, and a French pastry that one would purchase at a patisserie. Six in all. The order of the six was a mystery. They had to be ready for whatever category was thrown at them.

Reading the email and hearing Mr. Whisk's words were way different. Hearing him made the hair stand up on her arms. Fear mixed with excitement. She glanced around—were the others feeling the same?

Star had scoured Gran's recipes. They had numerous phone conversations before she settled on at least two variations for each category. She and Gran had joked that their choices would be the nucleus of Star's cookbook. The cookbook that the contest producers would see was published, maybe as an e-book to start, but hints that a major publisher may be waiting in the wings.

So, today was pie day. *Focus, Star. Breathe ... in ... out.*

Star's mind filled with the pie she had baked many, many times, even introduced to the diner, an American tradition if ever there was one—apple. She wondered if the other contestants knew the trick on how to insure the crust would not end up with a soggy bottom. Gran had impressed upon her, since the day Star began baking beside her, that a piecrust with a soggy bottom was a no, no. Maybe that would be her edge today.

What, what did he just say?

"Then the technical phase where the bakers are given a surprise recipe, pie, of course. Everyone will have the same recipe—the ingredients—but the recipe will be missing the instructions."

A groan escaped every baker's mouth.

"And finally, the show stopper. Your last chance to wow the judges. Your last chance to be named Star Pie Baker."

Thank God, I included two recipes for each episode. If I make it through today, I'll have to call Gran, add a third choice to each category.

"It is my honor to present your judges, two chefs from Miami. Each is a head chef at a five-star restaurant and known for their expertise in the kitchen, for their creativity and the fine taste of their recipes, and known as authors of best-selling cookbooks."

The two judges sauntered out from the doorway behind Jim—a man and a woman. A few bakers gasped recognizing the woman as an occasional guest on the Food Network—Suzanne Harting, a tall, slim woman with brown waves falling over her shoulders. Star wondered how she could remain so thin. She was known for *never seeing a stick of butter she didn't like.* The man, Chef Pierre Rouleau, was older, impeccably dressed in a tan blazer over black trousers, and what looked to Star as expensive black leather loafers with tassels. His salt and pepper hair set off his deep blue eyes and sexy smile—a killer guy with the Miami beauties Star surmised smiling back at him.

"Okay, bakers," Jim said spreading his arms wide. "Your best pie—you have two hours.

"Let the baking begin."

Chapter 20

CUTTING THE BUTTER, measuring and sifting the flour, crumbing the flour with the butter—Star worked quickly, methodically, adding the ingredients to the red mixer fitted with a flat blade. When the dough looked like crumbled cornmeal she slowly added cold water, pulsing the mixer just until the dough began to form a ball. She was in her element, blocking out everything and everyone around her. Everything except Jim's words, *must be baked to perfection*' kept running through her mind.

She heard her Gran, when Star was only eleven, telling her the dough had to be chilled making it easier to roll out.

Forming a rough ball, Star strode to the red refrigerator, sliding in the bowl holding the dough. While the dough chilled, she sliced the apples for the filling.

Checking her watch, she realized she was not keeping pace with her timetable.

"Grab the dough. Grab the dough," she muttered under her breath, urging herself to hurry. She must roll out the dough before it warmed, before it got too sticky to handle. *And*, she had the extra step, Gran's trick to prevent a soggy bottom—blind baking Gran called it. Bake the bottom crust separately.

Star positioned a portion of dough in the bottom of the fluted pie plate, laid a piece of silicon paper over it, and then poured dry baking beans to cover the paper. She popped the plate in the oven, setting the timer for ten minutes. It could take up to twenty so she had to watch it carefully, darting back and forth from the oven to the apple mixture for the filling.

Jim's voice cut through her focus. "Bakers, this is your one hour call. You have one hour left."

"Oh, no, no. I'm behind." Quickly surveying the other bakers, she only saw one pie plate with a piece of silicon paper hanging over the edge. Maybe, just maybe she had a chance to win this first test. Of course, the real test will come when the judges taste her pie, inspect the pie to determine if there is a soggy bottom.

Removing the plate from the oven, folding the paper into a packet, discarding the beans, she added the final ingredients to the sliced apples.

"Forty-five minutes remaining," Jim called out.

The air in the hall was filled with the aroma of baking pie crusts, of sweet filings. A mixture of apple, cherry and peach dominated.

Her heart was thumping as she tasted the mixture, adding a pinch more nutmeg. Scraping her apple mixture from the bowl, carefully laying the top layer of crust, cutting small slits in a flower petal pattern to vent the steam as the apples baked, she slid her pie into the oven.

Nothing more she could do but to watch it turn a golden brown, watch that it didn't burn, and pray that it would not have a soggy bottom. Sitting cross legged on the floor in front of the oven window, oven light on, she kept her vigil.

The room fell silent. Many of the other bakers were also sitting on the floor in front of their ovens.

Glancing at her watch, instinct told her it was time to remove her pie.

"Two minutes, bakers."

"One minute, bakers. Place your pie on the end of your station."

Doing as they were told, the bakers stood at attention behind their pies.

One after the other, the bakers took their pie to the judges to taste, to inspect.

Each judge pushed a fork in the entry, tasted, lifted the edge checking for a soggy bottom, made a few remarks.

The baker removed the pie, and the next baker advanced to the table holding the pie in oven mitts, placing the pie in front of the judges. And so it went.

Chef Suzanne complimented Star on the filling, perhaps a bit more cinnamon would be nice, and Chef Pierre complimented her on the crust—no soggy bottom.

The judges gave praise along with a mixture of harsh words. Only two pies received no feedback one way or the other.

Star felt she was in the running.

Jim and Stephanie huddled with the judges.

The verdict was agreed upon.

Jim, a dramatic pause, announced the decision of the judges.

Star came in first for her apple pie, receiving praise that the pie did not have a soggy bottom.

Jim asked the judges to retire to the back room as he handed out the recipe for the technical bake challenge.

A long table was set up on the stage with a framed picture of each baker standing in a row. The back of the pictures faced the judges when they returned. As they tasted, inspected each entry, they would *not* know who baked the pie they were judging.

Star was startled at the recipe Jim handed her. It was a pie. A meat pie. The ingredients were listed all right, but with only a few instructions. She felt like she had half a recipe, a hot water crust pastry. If only she could call Gran.

She remembered once her grandmother making a pork pie with diced carrots and celery. *Think, think, think, Star. The ingredients are here. But, how do I put them together. Hot water … no, use boiling water to melt the shortening. Roll it out between wax paper.* She worked feverishly as did the other bakers. She could hear Gran whispering instructions in her ear.

Time was called.

The bakers placed their pies on the long table behind their picture then stood back in a line as the judges entered.

Star knew her crust was too thick, pale not golden, and, oh my God, the crust had a soggy bottom. The only saving grace was the vegetables were cooked evenly.

She came in seventh.

The table was removed and they were given a thirty-minute break after which Jim again faced the bakers.

"Now the third and final pie bake—the show stopper. Your challenge is to bake thirty-six sweet tartlets. You have two and a half hours."

Star jerked strands of her hair under her visor's tabs, and set to work. She prepared and baked the crusts in mini-cupcake pans—three pans, twelve tartlets each.

The scent of melting chocolate, crystallized ginger, strawberry and other fruit mixtures circulated through the air.

Star was running out of time.

She began whipping together a delicate strawberry filling.

Concentrating, focused, she piped three small dollops of whipped cream on the top of each tartlet.

Chagrined, she looked at her product. The mini-crusts were not evenly filled with the strawberry delicacy, and there were larger dollops of cream on some and not so much on others.

Out of time, she had to go with what she had.

Time was called.

The judges made their choices.

One baker was sent home.

One was crowned Star Pie Baker, Episode One.

It was not Star.

Other than the one eliminated and the winner, she wasn't sure where she stood in the scheme of things, but she did know she would be back the day after tomorrow, Episode Two.

Jim made a final announcement. "There is a rule change. I am announcing the category for episode two ... Cakes.

"Jim," Stephanie whispered. "We have to talk."

Jim said goodbye to the bakers, praising them for their efforts, and reminding them they had the day off tomorrow but to return

Wednesday, 6:30 sharp. He waved to the judges, and the cameramen, thanking them for their participation.

Closing the door, he turned, bumping into his co-producer. "Sorry, Steph. Why the frown? Everything went well today. Fantastic actually. We have tomorrow to resupply the stations, to prep the studio—"

"I had a call from Lewis."

"Lewis, like in our financial backer?"

"Come on, Jim. This is serious. Lewis is having trouble nailing down the contract with the cable company for our amateur baker series."

"I thought they had signed."

"Apparently not!"

Chapter 21

A FEW DROPS of rain hit Tyler's windshield as he waited in the parking lot for Star. With the threat of rain he had pulled closer to the entrance. He watched as the front door swung open, groups of two or three stumbling out, one laughing, but most looked like they had been drawn through a ringer. One girl was crying.

Star emerged, shuffled toward the car. Tyler sprang out, running around to hold the door for her. No smile, she collapsed on the front seat. Back behind the wheel, he glanced out of the corner of his eye. *Was she eliminated?*

The rain picked up, the windshield wipers swishing the drops away.

Staring out the side window, Star sighed. "I'm still in."

"Hey, good news. Was it brutal?"

"Very. They film us every other day." She spoke slowly, exhausted monotone. "We have time to recoup our strength while the producers prep for the next episode—bring in fresh supplies, whatever we bakers need for the category. Today it was pies. Next—cakes."

"I thought they weren't going to tell you beforehand ... what category."

"Yeah ... well ... it's *cakes*."

"You, okay?"

Star nodded.

End of conversation.

Tyler pulled up to her apartment building and was about to turn the key off in the ignition. She turned to him. "I'm okay. Don't get out. Thanks for the lift ... see you tomorrow at the diner, one o'clock."

• • •

STAR FLOPPED ON her blowup-mattress, shoes and all. Closing her eyes, images of the bakeoff flashed in and out of her mind.

She woke with a start. Heart pumping. What time is it? I'm late. I'll be sent home.

She glanced at the clock. Eight. She'd passed out for two hours. Rolling off the mattress, she padded to the bathroom for a quick shower and then she had to call Gran.

Popping a frozen pizza in the oven, she opened a bottle of cheap red wine. Cheap or not, she wanted a drink. *Great, now I'm an alcoholic.* Finding the thought amusing, she began to feel her body gain some strength.

A couple of bites of the cheese pizza, a sip of wine, she reached for her cell.

"Gran, hi. It's me."

"Oh, sweetheart. I was about to call you. Talk to me."

"It was rough, Gran, but I lived to bake another day." Star laughed to herself. Now she was cracking jokes.

"Good for you. What's next?"

"Cakes. Gran, each episode is broken into three segments, three bakeoffs in the same category. Today it was pies ... by the way I came in first ... with the apple pie thanks to your trick. But the next two segments weren't so good. Good enough, however, so I wasn't sent home. Anyway, I need your thoughts—pineapple upside-down cake or your yummy German chocolate. What do you think?"

"The pineapple upside down can be tricky. You've made the German chocolate a lot. You could put a ribbon of butter cream in the center, or better yet a filling of the cooked custard and coconut you make so well ... a surprise for the judges when they cut into it. What about ganache frosting—a nice creamy chocolate? And pecans?"

"Our baking stations are setup with all the main ingredients we need, like flour, sugar. We even have a refrigerator. Gran, it's red. I'll take a picture with my phone. There's a large cupboard along the back wall of the studio with all kinds of stuff. I wrote down a quick inventory before I left today. I already thought about the German chocolate and I checked to be sure everything was available. Yes, they had pecans and semisweet chocolate bits. Heavy cream in the fridge."

"Then that's it. You're ready. Day after tomorrow. Call me. I love you, Star."

"Love you too, Gran. Thanks for the help."

Jotting a few notes, sipping her wine, her phone vibrated—a text message from Ash.

"Miss you. A."

"Made it through 1st round. S."

"OK 2 write story U in contest? A."

"Story OK. S."

"Wait for U tomorrow, 12:30? A."

"Perfect. Miss U 2. S."

• • •

TUESDAY

ASH MET HER at the usual spot—top of her block, the corner on Atlantic Avenue. Handing her a cup of strong coffee, no hot chocolate today, they began the short walk to the diner. They made plans for the evening. He'd be at the diner when her shift ended, and then he wanted to hear the details of the first filming, not just the quick synopsis she related as they walked. But he had enough for a short article he'd submit to the paper before the end of the day for tomorrow's edition. He read her the lead paragraph:

An amateur baking contest is being held on the outskirts of Daytona Beach. A local woman, Star Bloom, a short-order cook at Charlie's Diner, made it through the first round. The contest is being filmed for an upcoming reality TV series ...

Chuckling over his intro paragraph, she entered the diner. Wanda and Charlie immediately quizzed her for information on the bakeoff. Was there anything they could put on the diner's menu?

But it was Tyler she huddled with every chance they could squeeze in—any lull, or a quick back and forth at the order window. He pumped her for every detail on how the baking played out, then helped her with a strategy for the next bakeoff.

Her spirits lifted.

She was ready for *cakes*.

Chapter 22

BRIGHT SUNNY SKIES suddenly turned dark, shadowy, as storm clouds rolled over Volusia County. Intermittent thunderclaps were heard in the distance ... moving in rapidly. It was almost closing time when Ash ambled in taking his usual seat at the end of counter. He smiled at Star when she looked up from behind the order window, flashing him a wave.

Ty finished his sketch of the remaining two guests, as Star liked to call them. Scowling when he saw Ash, nonetheless, he set his drawing tablet down and offered Ash a cup of coffee. "Only the dregs left but you're welcome to it."

"No, thanks, Tyler. I'll just wait for Star."

"Suit yourself." Ty set the pot down, dumped the grounds, and commenced drawing a cartoon of Ash perched on the vinyl stool. He added a couple of horns, and a snarly look on his face. With a smirk, he tore the sheet from the pad, wadded it into a tight ball, tossed it in the trash can along with the coffee grounds.

Only two hours ago the silver diner was filled with sunshine and chatter from tourists new to the area, making plans for a weekend stroll on the beaches, browsing souvenir and T-shirt shops. Two by two they filled the booths, then the counter perching on the brown and white cowhide-patterned stools. Now, the last group staggered out, exhausted from a day of play.

The dinner guests had left.

Only Ash remained.

Charlie leaned against the wall, eyes closed, waiting to lock up. Wanda, her brows drawn together, caught the bent shoulders weighing on her husband. She leaned against the wall facing him, touched his arm. They spoke in hushed tones.

"Charlie, you can't keep taking the morning shift, waiting for Star to relieve you. We have to hire another cook and another waitress while we're at it. Business is picking up—seems like more tourists than ever. There are more families. The new menu items, along with Tyler's cartoons, are bringing them in. Lots more kids. We can't keep up this pace. Lucky we have Star and Tyler ... but we need help. If Star isn't eliminated soon, and I pray she isn't, the double shifts will kill you."

Charlie slowly drew in a breath, releasing it with a long sigh. He was tired and didn't have the heart to tell Wanda he wasn't feeling so good. "Yeah. You're right. Tomorrow, we can put a sign in the window. I don't want to hire just anybody. I couldn't take another cook like we had before Star came through the door."

A bolt of lightning struck nearby, turning night into day. Rolling thunder rocked the diner. The lights flickered but stayed on. A quick succession of lightning bolts flashed. Then came the driving rain.

Tyler looked up as a man entered the diner, his sweat suit soaked, a tattoo of a snake curling up his neck to chin. Flicking the rain off his arms, he stamped his feet. He walked up to the register, looked at the two leaning against the wall, looked at the girl behind the order window, then smirked at the goofball holding a pad next to the coffee station.

"Hey, you. Can I get a cup of coffee?" snake-man asked his eyes square on Tyler.

"Sorry," Tyler said. "We're just closing up. Come back in the morning, I'll give you a fresh cup ... on the house."

"Well, that's very hospitable of you, but you see I want it now. So I guess instead, if you would be so kind as to empty the register." As he muttered the words, he pulled out a pistol waving it at Tyler, then at Star stepping from behind the order window.

In a quick, smooth move snake-man grabbed her arm, spun her around in front of him, jabbing the gun to her temple.

"Hold on man, I'm going." Tyler quickly stepped to the register, tapped a key. The cash draw popped open. He picked up a handful of bills shoved them into the man's open hand around Star's neck, flexing his fingers.

"Get the rest. There's more," he yelled at Tyler squeezing his arm tighter around Star's throat.

Tyler emptied the drawer of the few remaining bills.

"That's it." Tyler's fingers ran around the drawer, showing there was nothing left.

Snake-man shoved Star into the coffeemaker, stuffed the bills into his pocket. He didn't see Ash leaping to her defense, lunging at him. Ash's arm whipped around the man's neck in a hammerlock. Defensively, snake-man swung his gun arm back striking Ash full force with the gun barrel, swirled around, dragging his fingers down Ash's face. Ash's body fell backward, his head smashing against the counter, legs buckling to the floor.

Snake-man, waving his pistol, backed away, backed into the Wurlitzer, backed out of the diner, retreating into the drenching rain, disappearing into the stormy night.

A lightning bolt shot through the sky, plunging the diner, the street into darkness.

Tyler fumbled in his pocket for his cell, tapped 9-1-1. "We need help. Charlie's diner, Atlantic Avenue, a robbery. A man's been hurt. Hurry."

"I have you, sir. There's an ambulance a block away. Stay on the line with me until you see them."

"Charlie, the flashlight, the shelf in back of you." Wanda inched back to where she last saw her husband.

A lightning bolt. Thunder.

Star stumbled to Ash lying lifeless. Kneeling beside him, she lifted his limp hand to her cheek. "Ash, Ash, can you hear me? Please, hear me."

"Got it." Charlie flashed a beam on his wife, on Tyler holding his cell out for light.

Tyler crouched beside Star, beside Ash's body, blood oozing from his skull.

"Ty, is he dying, is he—"

Ty leaned down, his cheek to Ash's nose. "He's breathing."

The 9-1-1- operator kept talking, asking something. "Stay with me caller. Do you see the medics?"

Charlie moved closer to Tyler and Star kneeling beside Ash, the flashlight's beam on Ash lying on the tiled floor, blood pooling around his head and shoulders.

An ambulance screeched to a halt.

"Yes, yes, I see them. They're here. Thank you. Thank you." Tyler disconnected the call.

Charlie stumbled to the door. Held it open.

Three medics charged into the diner with a stretcher. Knelt beside the unconscious man assessing his condition, lifted him onto the stretcher. "What's this man's name?"

"Ash," Star said.

"Ash what?"

"I ... I don't know."

The medics carried the unconscious man out the door strapped to the stretcher. "We're taking him to Halifax," the man at the foot of the stretcher yelled over his shoulder.

The medics drove away.

Star fumbled in the dark for Tyler's hand.

The storm raged outside.

Lightning struck somewhere across the street.

Claps of thunder.

Rain pelted the silver-aluminum diner through the howling wind.

The diner was dark except for a single beam from Charlie's flashlight pointed at his shoe.

Chapter 23

RAIN CONTINUED TO DRENCH Daytona Beach as Charlie peeled away from the diner heading to the hospital, Star sitting beside him. Tyler, remaining at the diner, continued to hold the door open, raindrops striking him as he stared at the disappearing van.

A lightning bolt snapped nearby, sending sparks in the air.

Tyler pushed the door closed, shutting out the storm. But he couldn't shut out the storm raging inside him, eating at his gut, eating at his heart. Hands out, he leaned against the door, beating the metal with his forehead.

Outside the street lights flickered on. Inside neon tubes circling the ceiling flickered to life.

Muttering, moving his hands to his hips, Tyler stared up at the greasy-film caking the ceiling.

"I'm losing her."

Thunder rocked the little diner again, neon flickered again then steadied, casting red and purple shadows.

Wanda called out. "Tyler, a black and white squad car, two officers coming up the walk. They must have been sent when you called 9-1-1 for help."

"I'm coming, Wanda."

Another lightning bolt struck somewhere off shore, sending a rumble of thunder overhead.

The first officer to step into the diner asked if everyone was okay. Wanda said yes, other than their customer being taken to the hospital. The officer explained they were on their way to an accident. A man blinded by the lightning hit a mailbox. Dispatch told them on the way to the accident they were to check on a robbery. A victim was being transported to the hospital. They were to make a quick assessment. Get a short statement, a description of the robber. Let them know an officer would be back in the morning unless more was required.

Tyler gave the officer a quick description of the man, a man with a snake tattoo up his neck.

The officer thanked him, rushed out the door.

Wanda and Tyler slumped on the counter stools in silence. As suddenly as it happened, it was over.

"Wanda, can I take you home? Mom watches the weather reports like a hawk. She insisted I drive her car today."

"Thank you, Tyler. You lock the front door. I'll clean out what's left in the cash register, and then let's get out of here."

The windshield wipers kept up their rhythmic dance but not the rain sloshing against the windshield faster than the wipers could slap it away. Even though the power was restored, Tyler drove slowly. Stopping at Wanda's house, he waited until she was inside. Seeing the front porch light flick twice, he headed home.

Climbing the stairs to his studio over the garage, he poured a glass of wine. Drank. He was in no mood to sip.

The intercom buzzed.

"That you, Tyler?" His mother's voice was hushed, comforting.

"Yeah, I'm home. Talk to you in the morning ... the car's fine. In the garage."

"Night, son."

Thunder rumbled overhead. Tyler ambled to the control panel, punched two buttons. Drapes over the window pulled to the side. Shades over the skylights rolled back.

Snatching the bottle of wine off the counter, he slid into the leather lounger, pushed the lever easing him back further.

"You're losing her you loser.

"Get real. You've already lost her.

"Superman? Oh yeah. Super dunce.

"What's Ash up to anyway. Always so mysterious. Shows up at the top of her street in the morning. Shows up at night to walk her home.

"Hey, loser, the woman isn't exactly complaining."

Pouring another glass of wine, Tyler, now shoeless, sockless, padded to his worktable, turned on his computer, fired up the animation software, and started drawing a cartoon of Ash.

It was night. He was dressed in black. Peering around a corner of an abandoned building. Gun raised.

"Nothing funny here," Tyler mumbled. "The way he flew at that robber … that takes commando training." The mouse gyrated across the screen—the man in black dove across the screen, off the screen.

"Star's not like him. She's sweet, trusting. He has no business pursuing her."

Ty began a new file. Inserted Star's cartoon image. A doll, big blue eyes, blonde curls. A Kewpie doll with a chef's hat.

Tyler smiled at her. Whispered. "You're bright, beautiful."

A frown spread across his face. "What can I do to make her see he's trouble? She doesn't belong with him.

"Nothing, stupid. There is nothing you can do."

Tyler opened the first of two cartoon stories he had just finished to send to Disney contractors. He had sent one to a studio in Burbank, California. He had planned to submit the second in the next few days—just a few more tweaks and it would be ready. The first company had replied almost immediately. They liked his work and would be in touch by the end of August. "Even if they don't hire me, maybe I should go to California … Burbank, where the action is."

He absent mindedly began a new cartoon. A golden yellow cat—Blondie—purring. A gray tabby—Sylvester—moves up to her, his grainy tongue caressing her ears. But wait, who is this? A black cat, yellow eyes, sidles up on tiptoe. Hisses. Scares Sylvester away. Blondie purrs up to Blackie, kisses him above his yellow eyes. He suddenly turns into a prince. She turns into a princess for her kindness. Sylvester slinks away.

"Shit, Sylvester. You loser."

Tyler shut down his computer.

Ran down the steps to the garage.

Dragging out his Harley, he took off, hoping the rain cleansing the night air would cleanse his mind of her.

Fat chance.

He yelled into the wind. "Just wait, stupid. It hurts too much to be close to her now. You have to pull back."

Returning home, parking the Harley, he raced up the stairs, three at a time. He turned on the computer, pulled up the dark cartoon of Ash, hit the delete button. Then deleted the Kewpie doll throwing him a kiss ... no ... not throwing him a kiss, throwing a kiss at Ash.

"You wait, Tyler.

"How long?

"Maybe forever ...

"But wait ... be there for her. Pick up the pieces when he leaves her."

Tyler's body ached to be with her, to be by her side for eternity.

God help him, he had fallen in love with the Kewpie doll.

Chapter 24

STREET LIGHTS WERE RESTORED, but lightning continued to strike sending thundering shockwaves overhead. Star peered through the windshield looking for downed power lines as Charlie sped along International Speedway. Leaning forward, she glanced at the clock on the dash—ten o'clock. An hour ago she had waved to Ash sitting at the counter waiting for her.

"We didn't ask which Halifax Hospital they were taking Ash to," she said wadding up her wet apron. It was drenched by the rain when she ran out of the diner to the van.

"I'm sure it will be the main hospital on Clyde Morris." Charlie glanced out at the rain, at other cars creeping along the flooded street. "Did you see that move Ash made on the robber? Like a street fighter, like he instinctively went for the kill. How did he do that?"

Star didn't answer. She was praying that Ash would be okay. His head was bleeding and he was still unconscious when the EMT's left. "I think he hit his head on the counter as he fell. The way he was struck, with the guy's fist holding the gun ... it was terrifying."

Charlie glanced sideways at Star. "Hey, he's going to be okay ... I think. That creep could have shot him ... could have shot you."

Charlie flipped his turn signal, turned onto Clyde Morris, then turned into the hospital's circular driveway. "I'll let you off at the emergency entrance, park the van. I'll find you."

Star nodded, unbuckling her seatbelt as Charlie pulled to a stop. Without a backward glance, she sprang from the van and darted through the emergency entrance, her eyes trained on the woman behind a window labeled *Information*.

"Hello, I'm looking for a man, just brought in by ambulance, unconscious, head bleeding. Where can I find him?" Star's breathing was erratic, tears forming as she spoke.

"Are you family?"

"No, I'm a friend. He has no family ... here."

"What's his name?"

"Ash ..."

The woman looked up. "Last name?"

"I ... I don't know ... he comes into the diner ... a regular ... we talk ... but..."

"Just a minute, let me check." The woman glanced at the telephone console, hit a button, then looked back at the young woman nervously rocking back and forth on the other side of the window. "Hi, Pete. Did you just admit a man with a head injury? May be unconscious, and—"

The woman paused, her eyes never leaving Star's face. "Yes. There's a woman here. Says she's a friend but doesn't know his last name ... sure. I'll send her down." She disconnected the call, cocked her head as she gave directions, pointing to a hall. Star turned, ran in the direction the woman had pointed.

A nurse stopped her in the hallway, led her into a brightly lit room with several beds. All were empty except two. A little girl was crying, a nurse cleaning blood from her arm, a man and woman hovering at the foot of her bed.

Star spotted Ash lying on his side three beds down. A doctor was examining the back of his head, a nurse standing beside him. Star quickly walked to the bed, to the doctor just as Ash moaned, regaining consciousness.

"Young man, you have a nasty gash on your head. Do you remember what happened?"

Ash looked around, only his eyes moving, trying to figure out where he was. Star moved to the head of his bed, slowly picked up his hand.

The doctor glanced over at her, finished his examination of the patient's head, easing the man onto his back.

"Hey, it's me, Star."

"S-S-Star. You okay? He ... ohhh."

She could barely hear him, barely understand what he was trying to say.

"What's your name, son?" The doctor flashed a penlight into one eye then the other, back and forth several times. "Pupils are dilated," the doctor reported to the nurse. "Get an X-ray of his head wound, stat."

"Your name, son?"

"Ashar."

"Your full name? Do you remember your last name?"

"Ashar Rais," he whispered.

"Can we contact your family ... so they won't worry?"

Ashar, Ashar Rais? Star wondered at his name. Why hadn't she ever asked him? They always just talked, using their first names, introductions with only first names. Crazy. She tried to think back—what had he told her? Actually, very little.

"No family," he mumbled. "Only Star."

A nurse entered the room, touched the doctor's sleeve. "Doctor, can you step out for a minute. Officer Watson would like a word with you."

"Sure. You just rest, Ashar. After we get that X-ray we'll know more about your injury. Your friend can stay with you."

The doctor quickly stepped away as Star leaned against the bed, Ash tightening his grip on her hand.

Ash said nothing. Brows drawn together, his eyes moved to Star, a nervous look veiling his face.

The doctor immediately returned with a uniformed officer by his side. "Seems you're a hero, Ashar. Charlie Armstrong said you saved this woman's life. This officer wants your take on what happened. I told him only two questions. I don't want you to talk much until we get the results of your X-ray."

"N-N-No." Ash squeezed Star's hand.

"It's okay, Ashar. It's okay." The doctor turned, led the officer out the door. "He's agitated. You'll have to question him later ... give us an hour ... after we know the extent of his head injury. He obviously didn't want to talk, could cause further damage if we force him. He did tell us his name, Ashar Rais. The woman said he had no family in the area, only her, a friend."

"The blonde woman by his bed?"

"Yes."

"Her name?"

"Sorry, I didn't ask," the doctor said.

"Okay, doc. Mr. Armstrong is her employer. He probably knows her name. I'll get his statement. Then, when you give the go ahead, I'll corroborate Armstrong's take of the robbery with Mr. Rais."

• • •

ASH CLOSED HIS EYES, his hand still gripping Star's hand. His eyes fluttered open. Dropping her hand, his fingers groped around his neck. "My, my chain ... Star ... my chain ... where? My mother's ring ... d-d-did they ... take it?"

Star looked up at the nurse preparing to wheel the bed to X-ray. "Excuse me. Did you, or the EMTs, remove my friend's gold chain? There's a ring on it. I've seen it. Plain gold band?"

"He didn't have it on when we wheeled him in. Let me ask the medics. I'll let you know when we bring him back from X-ray."

Star walked alongside him, continuing to hold his hand as three nurses guided the bed into the hall. "Don't worry, Ash. We'll find it and if that bad person took it, the police will find him. And ... I'll call Liz. Her husband is a retired Police Captain. He'll find out."

"N-N-No."

Star patted his hand. “Don’t worry. We’ll find it I’m sure.”

Dropping his hand, the swinging door shut in front of her, blocking her from continuing to walk by his bed to X-ray.

The bright hallway was empty.

Star took a step, then leaned against the wall. A tremor running through her body—her arms clutched her chest, holding her together. Closing her eyes, her thoughts filled with the terror she had felt, the robber’s arm pressing on her throat.

She lifted her hand, her fingers feeling her neck. The detective said Ash had saved her life. Her eyes shot open. She stared at the ceiling, stopping the re-enactment of the robbery—the fear, the gun.

Ash was so alone. She was his only friend. At least as far as she knew, and what she knew she was beginning to realize was precious little. He never talked about anyone else. Well, his grandmother … she had joked that her Gran believed in her too. Something they had in common.

He’s conscious. That’s a good thing. He knew who she was … that was good. The doctor, while concerned, didn’t seem to act as if his patient’s life was in danger. But Ash was afraid of something. What?

Her head back against the wall, eyes closed, mouth open, her breathing eased.

Well, whatever was bothering him, she was going to help.

Chapter 25

A ROUTINE REPORT was sent from the hospital to the Daytona Beach Police Department. Routine in the case of an assault—both the name of the victim and the perpetrator are included in the report. In the case of the diner robbery on Atlantic Avenue, the assailant was yet to be identified.

The officer on duty routinely runs the names through the Florida State database--past felons on file, current persons of interest, as well as those listed as wanted. Hearing a beep, the second-shift officer put down his tuna fish sandwich, wiped mayonnaise from the corner of his mouth, and scanned his monitor.

There was a hit. A name on the hospital report matched a name on file in Tallahassee.

Ashar Rais. His student visa had expired. He was in the country illegally. But, what sparked the officer's interest was the country of origin—Syria.

Within seconds, the information was relayed to Homeland Security in Washington, D.C.

Agent Donovan, FBI, was working late when the alert crossed his screen. The alert had originated from the Daytona Beach Police Department. Subject: a Syrian man in Florida on an expired visa. Donovan's fingers hit the keys on his keyboard, immediately mining the Homeland Security database for the name: Ashar Rais.

A ping. An alert. There was a match to a name on file.

Donovan quickly made two telephone calls.

The first call he placed to the Chief of Police, Daytona Beach, his private line, confirming the receipt of DBPD's alert and in turn relaying to DBPD this new piece of information—surname of Rais matched a family being monitored in Syria by the agency. Donovan asked the Chief if, after looking into the expired visa, in his opinion, did the situation fall under deportation guidelines? The Chief said he would check. The two lawmen chatted a few minutes ending with a quip from the chief that the agent should go home and go to bed.

Donovan placed the second call to Manny Salinas, a private investigator he trusted. "Hi, Manny, hope I didn't wake you."

"No, Liz and I got caught up in a late-night rerun—NCIS Miami." Manny chuckled. "What's up." Manny turned his head, talking softly. Liz was curled up on the couch next to him. Her legs stretched out, bare feet in his lap.

"The visa of a man in Daytona Beach. He's at the Halifax Hospital with a head injury. His name came up on Florida's law enforcement database in Tallahassee—expired student visa. Second hit happened at my end—last name of Rais matched the name of a couple of men we're tracking in Syria. A father and son. Please dig into this guy. I'm sending you some info on him. I just talked with the DB police chief—told me to go to bed. Said he was a friend of yours, worked with you before you retired. He'll be calling you ... said he always appreciates your help, shorthanded shit. I guess you're on some sort of a retainer with the department?"

"Yeah. Private Investigator. I'll check out this Rais fellow. Do you think he might be linked to the chatter you called about a few days ago?"

"Don't know—that's why I'm calling you. And, Manny, I want to keep a lid on this. Don't want to spook him ... if there is a connection."

"I hear you."

"Let me know what you find out."

"I will. Bye." Manny laid his cell phone on the end table. Looking at Liz he was overwhelmed with his love for her, his need to protect her. He wanted only happy thoughts swirling around the baby she was carrying. His baby.

Chapter 26

WEDNESDAY

A SHARP STRIP of bright light from the hallway punctuated the shadowy hospital room. Groggy with pain medication, Ash lazily scanned the room. The digital clock displayed 2:01 a.m. He had been moved from Emergency to another room. The bed next to him was not occupied. His eyes returned to Star. Her hair hung loose in golden waves when she discarded the band holding it in a ponytail. The waves fell forward covering her face as she slept, slumping from the chair onto his hospital bed, her fingers relaxed lying over his hand.

A wave of warm emotion flowed through him. He had never known a woman to show such caring. He permitted the warmth to linger, engulfing him, wrapping him safely in a cocoon free from harm. *Could this be love?*

Chatter from passing attendants in the hall snapped him out of his dream state. The feelings were not real, and, more important, he knew he could not allow himself such a lapse from reality. He carefully pulled his hand from under hers.

Star felt the movement, looked up with a timid smile. She tucked a wayward strand of hair from her face. "How do you feel?"

"Like I've been hit with a brick." His thumb ran over her fingers, his eyes scanning her face. She was tired.

"I heard the doctor tell your nurse that you have a concussion. He said a day in the hospital, another test, and then, barring something unforeseen, you should be able to leave."

Ash gently touched the strand of hair that fell forward again over her cheek. "You must have been scared. You should go home. Get some rest."

"I was. You were something else, the way you came after that guy. You'd think you rescued people from danger all the time," she said with a soft giggle.

"I'm just glad you're all right. Really, you should go ... but how—"

"I will in a little while. Charlie brought me. We followed the ambulance. He just left. I texted Ty, asking him to pick me up at six—sunrise." Another giggle. "Episode two of the bakeoff is this morning."

Alarm spread across Ash's face. "The competition ... how can you? You're exhausted."

"That's what coffee is for ... lots and lots of coffee. I put in an order with Ty—two large, high-test mugs of coffee. I was waiting for you to wake up. Silly me, I fell asleep. Do you want some water? I can get some ice cubes down the—"

"Water would be great. But first, can you do something for me?"

"Sure. What would you like?"

Her voice was soft, vulnerable. Ash hesitated, but he needed help. "If I'm here for a day, I could be in trouble."

"Ash, don't even think such a thing. The police officer said you were a hero."

"I need you to call my grandmother in London. Is there some paper—ooh."

"Hurts when you move your head?"

"Yeah, a little. Reminder—the brick. Do you have paper? I'll give you her number. Tell her what happened and that I'm in the hospital. She'll understand, know what to do. What time is it?"

Star turned so the light fell on her watch. "Wow, I really conked out. It's almost two-thirty."

"Okay, that makes it eight-thirty in the morning in London. Better yet, do you have your cell? My clothes, and stuff ...they must have taken everything. My cell was in my pants pocket."

"Yes, I have mine."

"Please, make the call now. We should catch her in her apartment. When she answers tell her I'm calling and hand the phone to me. Is that okay?"

"Yeah, sure."

"She'll feel better if she hears my voice."

Ash slowly dictated the country code, followed by his grandmother's telephone number in London.

Referring to the piece of paper, Star tapped the numbers, mouthed to Ash that the phone was ringing. Then her brows went up. "Hello. Hello, my name is Star Bloom. I'm with your grandson Ash, Ashar. Hang on I'm handing the phone to him."

Star watched and listened as Ash briefly explained to his grandmother what happened. That he was in the hospital, a bump on the head, insisting that it was nothing. Still, the doctor was taking precautions and was running some tests. "Grandmother, I gave my name to the police ... of course, they asked. They said I was a victim of an assault. My friend Star, she's with me. She heard the doctor say I'll be out of the hospital in a day—after another test."

Ash finished the explanation, listened to his grandmother's response and then said goodbye. Disconnecting the call he closed his eyes, breathing out a puff of air in relief.

"Is she okay ... with what you told her?" Star picked up her cell phone that he held in his palm resting on the sheet.

"Yes. She's catching a flight as soon as she can."

"Coming now? You seem to be worried. I'll call Manny, Liz's husband ... you know, the retired police officer. Maybe he can—"

"N-n-no. He won't un-un-understand."

"Why are you stuttering?" *He's acting like he did something wrong, which is crazy. He saved my life.*

"I-I-it happens sometimes."

Star went down the hall for ice. She was relieved he asked for her help, but at the same time uneasy. It was like he opened a door just a crack for her, and then closed it once she did what he wanted.

The good thing was that he seemed to be gaining strength. Maybe it was just a nasty bump on the head. But then why would his grandmother be in such a rush to fly to Florida? Such a long trip. There must be more to it.

Star liked the way he looked at her just now. Maybe after the competition they could spend more time together ... alone.

She rubbed her eyes. She was beyond tired. Perhaps someone at the nurses' station could show her where she could take a shower. She sure needed one. That would help to revive her. Today was another big day. She had to push through the exhaustion. A couple more hours and Ty would be here, pick her up, take her to the competition, and, most important of all, bring her coffee.

Chapter 27

SUNRISE!

Star stepped out into a new day refreshed after a hot shower, even though she still wore the clothes from yesterday. As promised, Ty was in front of the hospital, his mom's Lincoln purring like a kitten, waiting for her to slide in.

Ducking his head to see through the side window, Ty smiled, waved, leaned over to open the door. His lips turned up at the corners, but his eyebrows were drawn together in worry lines. How could she possibly bake today, let alone compete? Cakes shmakes—she's exhausted.

"Two coffees, high test, Miss Bloom." Ty nodded to the cup holders in the console as she dropped her tote on the floor mat, her feet straddling the bag as she sat down.

"Did anyone ever tell you that you're a life saver?"

"Orange ... cherry?"

"I'm serious, Ty. Do you want one of these coffees?"

"Nope. Both yours, and there's a bag of clothes for you on the backseat." Ty shot her a grin as he turned onto Williamson Boulevard.

"Clothes?"

"When I told mom what happened ... she dragged a complete replay out of me including your staying at the hospital. Of course, she knew you would be heading straight to the bakeoff. Anyway, you two are the same size—her words not mine. Personally I think your body is curvier—"

"Tyler Jackman, you know nothing about my ... my curves."

"Not true, my little Kewpie doll. I presume there's a restroom at the studio so you can change. Mom couldn't decide on skirt or trousers. I told her you wore slacks and a blouse for the first episode."

"Please, thank her for me. I didn't know what to do and it was too late to ask you to stop by my place when I realized I was a mess. I did take a shower thanks to a nurse who took pity on me. I spilled an egg yolk, as you can see ... Ty, that was so scary..." suddenly gasping for air she began to hyperventilate.

"Drink your coffee, Miss Bloom. Now! Drink!"

She did as she was told. After a few sips she was okay. Closed her eyes, leaned back.

"Did you recognize the man, Ty. Ever seen him before?"

"No to both questions. You?"

"No. At least I don't think so."

"I made a quick sketch of him—when he walked in. Big guy. Sweats were too small—sleeves were above his wrists. And, there was that tattoo."

Sitting up, Star thought a moment. "I didn't see a tattoo. What was it?"

Tyler didn't want to go back to that moment. He was so scared the man was going to hurt her. "A snake on his neck. So, How's Ash?"

"OK. Doctor said he was OK, unless..."

"Unless?"

"Unless something shows up on the X-rays. He woke up within minutes after Charlie and I got to the hospital. Then early this morning, the first thing he asked ... was I OK. Then he asked me to call his grandmother. He talked to her. I didn't. Ty, she's flying to Florida. She might even land by tonight. Ash seems to be scared of something ... he began to stutter.

"Yeah? Like scared of what?"

"I don't know. Well, like when the police officer came into his room, and ... when I said I'd call Manny if he needed help. Help for what ... I haven't a clue."

"Well, Miss Star Bloom, it's show time. Episode two ... I believe you mentioned something about a cake. Save me a piece."

"I'll see what I can do."

"An officer Fred Watson—" Ty began to say, but Star cut in.

"Fred Watson. That was the officer who came to talk to Ash at the hospital. Never did ... last night anyway. The doctor wouldn't let him stay when Ash became agitated."

"Well, he's coming to question Charlie, Wanda, and me at eight this morning."

"Give him your sketch. I bet you captured a pretty good likeness of the man ... before he drew his gun."

Ty turned into the driveway, parking in front of the studio. Running around the car, he opened the door and squatted looking up at her. "Are you okay?"

"Yeah. Really, I'm fine. All right with you if I take this other coffee with me?"

"It's yours. Come on, out you go." He grasped her hand, took the coffee as she shouldered her bag. "Hang on ... the clothes. Mom would kill me if I didn't give them to you. Hey, what about your Gran's recipe book?"

Star patted her tote. "Right here. I kept looking up stuff yesterday between grill orders. When Charlie drove me to the hospital I grabbed my tote—everything was in it—purse, recipe book, hair brush. But, no change of clothes," she said smiling.

Seeing her smile, seeing her standing, spine beginning to stiffen, he was relieved. What a woman. He handed her the bag of clothes and gave her a quick hug. "I'll be back at six. Text me if there's a change. And now, Miss Bloom, go kick ass."

"Yes, sir. Thanks."

Ty waited for her to enter the building along with two other contestants. Inhaling, he puffed out his cheeks in a long, drawn out sigh.

Chapter 28

LUGGING IN THE groceries from the car Manny heard Liz call out to put the bags on the counter and to please give each dog a biscuit.

The canines, Peaches and Maggie sat on the wrap-around porch by the backdoor, tails sweeping the leaves away as the master of the house hauled in the last of the grocery bags.

"Yeah, yeah, I see you. Come on girls. Mama says to give you a biscuit. Don't know why, you just had breakfast."

Entering the kitchen he gave Liz a peck on the cheek, put the final two bags on the counter, and held out a biscuit to Peaches, then to Maggie—all in that order.

"Want some coffee, Manny? I could sure use a cup. I'm a little tired."

"I'll get it. You go in the living room, sit tight."

Liz giggled. "I feel wonderful, but I'll let you pamper me now while I can enjoy it, before I get mean and cranky."

"Love of my life, you could never be mean or cranky. There's a half a pot left from this morning. I'll zap it and be right in. Turn on the nine o'clock news, please."

"Will do." Liz leaned back in her lady-recliner and flipped the television to the local news. The pretty reporter was standing in front of Charlie's Diner gravely relating the story of the attempted robbery the night before.

"Hey, Manny, come here. Quick."

Manny hustled in plopping down in his man-size recliner after setting Liz's coffee cup on the table next to her chair. "What?"

"Look ... it's the diner. Star's diner. There was a holdup last night. That young man she introduced Jane and I to in the driveway, Ash I believe she said his name is, was hospitalized with a possible concussion. He's still there, the hospital, but ... may be released tomorrow. We should go ... see if there is anything we can do. Don't you think? Get the real skinny."

"What did the reporter say his name was?"

"Ashar Rais ... I think ... unusual. Let me call Jane. Maybe she'd like to go to lunch with us. Okay with you?"

"Ah, I have to see the chief. He called last night ... you were asleep. He wanted my thoughts on a case. You go ahead if Jane's free, otherwise wait for me. Maybe we'll go tomorrow."

"Silly, since when is Jane not free for lunch."

"Okay, but be careful. Is your cell charged?"

"Manny, I'll drive very slowly and yes my cell is charged. You're spooking me out. If your meeting with the chief doesn't take long, text me. If there's time, you can still join us at the diner."

Chapter 29

STRUGGLING TO FOCUS on her three-layer German chocolate cake, her go-to-cake, her personal best, Star kept a picture in her mind of when she was a little girl. She and Gran wore matching white bib-aprons, ruffled at the bottom. Together they had mixed the batter, poured the batter into three cake pans, and popped the pans into the oven. Then they licked their spatulas coated with the chocolate batter. Holding on to that image was the only way she blocked out the robbery, the gun, Ash lying on the floor. She did let in one thought—Ty picking her up this morning with two coffees and the thoughtfulness of his mother.

Keeping Gran's image front and center, also helped to block out the commotion around her. The young man, still assigned to the baking station behind her, cursed up a storm. She thought she heard him say his cake was burned, mixed with a barrage of expletives. Star turned slightly and with a quick glance confirmed his frustration was valid. She saw the white cake with a definite charred edge.

The young man was slathering on thick chocolate frosting, trying to hide the burned spots. She wondered if the judges would catch the error. It depended on where they cut for their taste test.

The only amusement during the bakeoff came when Jim Whisk announced the recipe for the Technical Challenge, the recipe with no directions. Pineapple Upside Down cake. The cake she and Gran had gone over before switching to the German

Chocolate. Today's final bake-off: thirty-six cupcakes, baker's choice of flavor.

Star came in fourth at the end of the day. She was OK with fourth considering she was lucky she showed up at all.

Packing up her things, she headed for the door. The young man was still cursing—he had been eliminated. What she didn't expect were two other baker women in an agitated conversation, to the point of hysteria, at the back of the room with Jim Whisk and Stephanie Hall. One of the women, tears rolling down her cheeks, the other's face so red Star thought she would explode. Before stepping out the door she thought she heard them say they were withdrawing, the stress was too intense, they couldn't take it.

Pausing, she looked back at the huddle. Did she hear them right? They were pulling out of the competition? Heads together, Jim and Stephanie nodded in agreement, the two stressors thanking Jim for the opportunity to compete in the bakeoff.

Turning away, Star wondered at the implications. Three leaving meant there were six bakers left.

Tomorrow was an off day and thank heavens for that. She sorely needed time to regroup, to gain some perspective on what happened at the diner, and what happened to Ash. Time to unscramble her head and above all get some sleep.

Friday was scheduled to film Episode three. This time Jim had announced the category: *cookies*.

Chapter 30

STUNNED, JIM AND STEPHANIE stood watching the two women leave. With the eliminations, and the two women withdrawing, they were down to six competitors.

"Steph, I don't know about you but I could use a drink," Jim said loosening his tie, unbuttoning the top button of his white shirt.

Stephanie sighed. "Sounds good. We have some serious issues to discuss. Let's go back to the motel, meet in the bar. We can get something to eat. I'm not sure I can swallow anything, but I'll have to try."

Twenty minutes later the pair sat across from each other, staring down at the stuffed olives in the bottom of their martini glasses, the red dot in the olives, bloodshot eyes, staring back at them.

After a long sip, a drawn out sigh, Jim leaned forward. "Any word from our backer, about the network signing our show?"

"Nothing positive. A lot of mumbo jumbo about redoing the winter programming schedule. Jim, I wonder if he's playing us. Do you think we should close down the project?"

"Steph, how can you even suggest that?"

"Not so loud."

Jim sat back, his hand swiping over his bald head. "All the money we've sunk into the show, the bakers ..."

"Oh yeah, the bakers. Shit, we're down to six," Stephanie said hunching over her drink glaring at him.

"Well, look at the positive side."

"What's that? I'd like you to tell me something positive." Stephanie flagged the waiter, waving at their glasses for refills.

"Maybe our backer will have the contract by the end of the week. Six contestants means we cut down the restocking of the baker's stations. Plus, I was thinking today ... how we might tighten the production, the schedule. Naturally, it was before the two lame-Os withdrew."

"Go ahead, talk to me. Tell me about all this creative thinking." She stabbed an olive, glanced away.

"Tighten the schedule. We're down to six. We could have a double elimination, and then film the finals with four bakers. We already planned on three bakers for the finals so what's one more?"

"Go on." Stephanie slid their empty glasses to the waiter as he set down their refills.

"No more days off between episodes—except for tomorrow of course. Think of it. Two episodes, two categories. Say ... cookies and the final round—candy."

"I see where you're going. My God, Jim, that would mean we only pay through Saturday—the building rental, the equipment rentals, supplies, and the camera crew. We could almost make it."

"Yeah. And heat up the excitement—people withdrawing because of stress, crying, all kinds of drama. Heck, we could wrap it all up with money to spare, *and* a contract by the end of the week."

"Okay. Episode three stays as is on Friday. We announce the change before the baking begins, but we'll also announce that it's the semifinals—added pressure."

Jim smiled, squinting gleefully. "Yeah, added pressure, drama, and the finals will be filmed the next day on Saturday. We can pitch it as saving them money ... those who are staying in motels. And, those who took time off from work can get back to their jobs."

"We feel their pain." Stephanie chuckled. "They can go home, tell their families what a great experience they had making it to the finals—"

"And we have ourselves a reality show—signed, sealed and delivered." Jim sat grinning across the table at his co-producer.

"Well, that means stirring up some media buzz, start hyping Saturday's finals. Shit, I have to get on it tomorrow. Invite the press ... Friday and Saturday ... semi's and finals. We should warn the cameramen, the movers that Saturday will be the end. Who knows, maybe the AP will pick up the story."

Jim looked up. "Steph, we have to be careful. Everything may still work out and we don't want to cause confusion about the competition not proceeding as advertised or, God forbid, possibly being cancelled. Go ahead with your idea—media on Friday and Saturday." Jim signaled the waiter. "Can we get some pretzels over here?"

"Oh, I forgot to tell you. A local reporter called. Wants to write a follow-up story and take pictures. Do you think Friday, or Saturday. Maybe both." Steph nodded to the waiter, pushed the bowl of pretzels to Jim.

"Same reporter who wrote the first story?"

"No. Another one."

"I changed my mind. Media on Saturday only. Okay, Co-producer in charge of press releases, let's see what you're made of. Start calling tomorrow—TV, radio, newspapers—invitation only to the finals on Saturday. If they ask about the semi's, tell them the bakers are too stressed out. Invitation is for Saturday."

"Jim, we originally planned a big celebration party after the winner is announced ... a picnic outside, balloons, drinks. The celebration was described in the original package we sent to the bakers. Eliminated bakers are invited back, as well as all friends and families. A great photo op for the final scene. But ... we have to scale back. We don't have the money for such a grand plan. What do you want to say ... to the bakers, the media?"

"Nothing. We say nothing. We'll scale back from a BBQ to soft drinks and don't forget, candy is the category for the finals. Of course the bakers don't know that yet. What could be better—soft drinks, candy, and a winner, and the bakers' families and friends. Go ahead, add balloons. Finals always have balloons. We'll go all out."

"Here's to you, partner, and all that creative thinking." Stephanie raised her glass, flagged the waiter, calling out to bring a couple of menus. She was starving.

Chapter 31

THURSDAY

THANKFULLY SHE HAD a day off from the competition. Star rubbed her forehead, trying to put at bay the onslaught of a monster headache. Thursday was lining up to be a killer of a day. No time for lollygagging, she rolled off the mattress, sprang upright performing a few touch-her-toes.

She padded to the bathroom, giving Mr. Coffee a punch as she passed. Shrugging off the white T-shirt she slept in, she stepped into the shower. Leaning into the hot steamy water, hands against the tile, thoughts of the last few days tumbled through her brain.

The knot in her stomach returned. If only she could make sense of it all. Ash suddenly stuttering. His grandmother winging her way to his side. If his grandmother was so concerned why not his mother or father?

The wound on his head wasn't life threatening, at least the doctor didn't seem to think so or he wouldn't be talking about discharging him from the hospital today. But something was bothering Ash or he wouldn't have called his grandmother in the first place, and he certainly didn't try to dissuade her from coming.

Maybe she'd learn more today, get a better picture of Ash when she meets his grandmother, if she meets her. And hopefully the knot in her stomach would ease except her neck was still sore. A grim reminder of the robbery.

Turning off the shower, she stepped out grabbing a towel. Smiling at her image in the fogged up mirror, she thought of Ty's cartoon. Kewpie doll—*NOT*.

She dressed, going over the first few hours at the diner in her mind as she gulped a mug of strong coffee, being careful not to spill.

Liz and Manny had rescheduled their visit to the diner to this morning when they learned she'd be there. Jane couldn't make it—something about an appointment to touch up her hair's pink glow.

Then there was Detective Watson—he was coming this morning to go over everyone's statements.

She'd texted Charlie back and forth about manning the grill this morning—not this afternoon. And, could she borrow the van around noon to go to the hospital? His final text—*yes to all*. Star chuckled. Charlie didn't like texting. He kept his messages short and sweet.

Cookies, cookies, cookies. She made a mental note to go over bakeoff number three with Gran.

Leaving her apartment for the diner, Star instinctively looked for Ash waiting for her at the corner, hot chocolate in hand. But, of course, he wasn't there today.

The morning started slowly, picking up just as Liz and Manny arrived. Charlie gave her ten minutes to meet with them, then he wanted her back on the grill.

Liz popped out of the booth, gave her a hug, scanning her head to toe to make sure she was okay, the two sliding back in facing Manny across the table. Star thought Manny was preoccupied, but when she mentioned that Ash thought the robber had yanked off the chain from around his neck, he took note of what she was saying.

"Did Ash give you a description of the chain?" Manny wanted to know.

"Gold, with his mother's gold ring strung on it. His grandmother is flying in ... from London. The nurse gave him his phone—he texted me that she called, told him she'd be at the hospital about noon."

Star smiled up at Tyler as he set three coffees on the table. "Hey, good—"

She was interrupted as Detective Fred Watson sauntered in, walked up to their booth. "Nice. Everyone I want to chat with held captive in a booth."

Tyler grinned at the detective. "Sir, I added to the drawing I gave you. The whole robbery—frame by frame—the gun, Ash flying through the air, Star in the grips of the bad guy, and snake-man's snarl demanding I give him the money from the register. It's all here." Tyler pulled a folded sheet from his pocket, laid it on the table, smoothing the edges.

"Manny, I bet you wished when you were a cop on the beat that you had an eye-witness like Tyler here.

"For sure. Tyler, can I have a copy of that sketch?"

"Right here, Investigator," Tyler said pulling another folded sheet from his pocket, handing it to Manny. "See, Detective Watson, his sweats are too small for him, sleeves didn't reach his wrists. And ... and, there was this tattoo, the head of a snake crawling up his neck from under the black sweat suit. And ... he's standing in front of me demanding that I give him the cash—he's taller than me. Almost a head taller. Just so you know, I'm six-feet ... exactly." The cartoon illustrated a white man with a blondish brown curl sticking out from under the sweat suit hood.

"Fred, Star was telling Liz and I that her friend's grandmother will be with him at the hospital, noon, flying in from London," Manny said.

Liz looked from the detective to Manny. A message passed from one man to the other, their eyes, and she didn't think it had to do with Ty's cartoon.

"Is that so? Well, I'll make it a point to be there. Still need to go over his statement."

"Star, I need you at the grill," Charlie called through the order window.

"Be right there. Well, duty calls. Talk to you later, Liz. We didn't get much of a chance."

"Yeah, Star. We'll talk." Liz said the words to Star but she was exchanging wide eyes with her husband.

"What?" Manny knew the what. That wife of his never missed a thing and several interesting pieces of information had dropped into that pretty head of hers. If he had to guess what was on her mind, it was a stop at the pawn shop down the street.

"Excuse us, folks," Manny said inching out of the booth, offering his hand to Liz. "We have a few errands to run. Catch you later, Fred, and best of luck, Star ... the competition. Tyler, you're a natural. I have a feeling the DBPD will be calling you."

"Why? For what?"

"Whenever they have an eye witness ... asking you to sketch the witness's description."

"Bye, all." Ignoring Manny's hand, Liz scooched out of the booth, headed out the door with a wave over her shoulder to Star.

Chapter 32

"STITCH. HOLD UP. What's your hurry?"

"Oh, let's see. Where to begin."

Clicking the locks on their black SUV, Manny held the door open for his wife. Liz flounced in, made a big deal of putting her shoulder bag on the floor of the backseat as the door shut.

Manny decided to wait it out. She would let loose soon. She never could hold anything in for very long.

"What do you think? Stop at Eddie's Pawn Shop? See if that gold chain was pawned there?"

"Capital idea." Liz smoothed out the crease in her slacks, the motion that always drove him crazy. He liked a military crease in his trousers. "And, if Eddie doesn't have it, the next one down the street may. Both are close to the diner. Petty cash from the register ... snake-man, as Tyler called him, is probably a local."

"Tyler's drawing was priceless—a gold ring strung on a gold chain, a tall guy with a snake up his neck. Easy to ID. We've both used Eddie as an informant. He'll tell us if the chain was pawned at his shop in the last thirty-six, forty-eight hours or so. An item like that burns a hole in a petty thief's pocket—too hot to keep for long." Manny glanced at his wife. She was about ready to blow. Best if they talked to Eddie first.

Manny pulled up in front of Eddie's Pawn Shop, ducked his head to see out the window if the shop was open. He knew Eddie opened at seven. He was stalling to see if Liz was ready to talk. Turning the key off in the ignition, both doors of the SUV were flung open at the same time as the private eyes, always dressed from head to toe in black, strolled into the shop.

"Elizabeth, Manny, my two favorite snoops. Let me guess. You didn't come for tea?"

"You got that right, Eddie," Liz said.

"Any customers this morning, Eddie," Manny asked perusing one of the showcases.

"Customer, no. Wanna-be customer? Maybe. Depends on what you mean."

"Robbery Tuesday. Late. Tall guy in a black sweat suit, soaked. It was raining. That sound like one of your customers?" Liz flashed her megawatt smile. Her smile always got to Eddie.

"As I said, Elizabeth, it depends. Yada, yada. A man came in with a piece of gold yesterday. I couldn't accommodate him."

"Where did you send him, Eddie?" Manny asked without looking away from the showcase.

"Al's, down the street."

"Okay, well, if a customer comes in wanting to pedal a gold chain with a ring going dingle dangle, give us a call. Here's another card to put with the last one I gave you." Liz pulled a card from her pants pocket, swore under her breath, handed him her card.

Back in the car, Manny pulled away from the curb. "What's with the swearing back there?"

"Pants are getting tight."

They hit pay dirt at Al's—*Pawn It Here, Best Prices*. Liz took several photos from different angles of the chain and ring with her cell phone, a close-up of the lettering around the inside of the gold band. Arabic lettering. A woman's ring.

"Detective Watson will be by. He'll want to see this. Evidence in a robbery. Best if you take good care of this chain and ring. Don't let it out of your sight, if you know what I mean," Manny added.

Back in the car, Manny decided on a course of action. "I'll drive by the house. Let the dogs run." He was hoping Liz would let off the steam that was still inside her if she was home.

He knew his wife. They no sooner stepped through the backdoor when Liz turned on him.

"Are we partners, or are we not partners?"

"Stitch—"

"No, no ... not Stitch. Elizabeth Stitchway Salinas, Private Eye ... TRUSTED PI. Yes?"

"Yes, but—"

"You're holding out on me, Manny. What was all that googly-eye stuff going on between you and Fred back at the diner?"

Manny swiped his hand over his head. "I told you the chief called last night."

"About a case you said."

"Yeah, well he called about a guy here on an expired visa."

"So?"

"So the guy's name is Ashar Rais. Ashar as in Ash. He's the same person who was hospitalized as a result of the diner robbery."

"You mean Ash as in Star's friend?"

"Looks like it. And there's more. Donovan called."

"As in Alex Donovan, FBI? That Donovan?"

"Yes. He wanted me to nose around, quietly, as in don't tell anyone. The name Rais came up with a match when he did a Homeland Security search ... after the expired-visa person popped up."

"My God, Manny. Is Ash a terrorist?"

"Elizabeth, as your husband, not as your business partner, I'm going to protect you, and if that means keeping you, my wife ... and child ... out of harm's way ... keep my bullheaded wife from charging into danger, then that's what I, Manny Salinas, husband and father-to-be will do."

"Damn. Not fair, Manny. I'm throwing a yellow flag. I can't fight the daddy card."

Manny quickly closed the distance between them, wrapped her in his arms, tucking her sparky red curls under his chin. "Truce?"

Shrugging. Sighing. "Okay, truce. Now, can we go see Ash? Meet his GM?"

"You drive a hard bargain, Stitchway."

The dogs, Peaches a black lab mix, and Maggie a black and white border collie mix, were lying by the backdoor, heads on paws, eyes switching one to the other as their humans spoke.

"Give the girls a biscuit. Let 'em out," Manny said. "I can't take their sad eyes. I'll go call the DB Chief, and Donovan and Fred. Tell them what we found. Emphasis on WE! Then we go to the hospital."

"Manny. Come here," Liz said sweetly.

She stood on her tip toes, brushing her lips across his moustache. "I love you."

"Umm, your pants *are* a little tight, partner."

Chapter 33

ASH WAITED, HIS EYES riveted on the doorway to his hospital room.

It was Noon.

His grandmother, the only person he trusted as far back as he could remember, back to his fourth or fifth year. She was the one who raised him. At first weekends, a month now and then, but after his mother died, his mother's mother came for him. She took him away to live with her and his grandfather in London. It was at her knee that he learned compassion, at their knees that he turned away from violence.

A nurse in blue scrubs entered his room, smiled, took away the lunch tray. People passed by the door as he waited—doctors, nurses, visitors, a bed pushed by three men in scrubs, an IV strung to the patient's arm—young, old? He couldn't tell.

A woman with gray hair, clipped back, stepped in the doorway, framed in the doorway. A warm, loving smile spread to her lips, her eyes.

"Ashar ... I am here." She walked to him, her arms open wide to him.

Flinging his feet loose of the bed sheet, Ash stood receiving her embrace.

Looking into his eyes, she scrutinized his face. "Ashar, you are well?"

"Yes, Grandmother. I'm okay. A slight cut on my head. Here, sit." He pulled a chair close to his bed, settled her into the chair.

Pushing a pillow aside he sat cross legged on the bed holding her hands.

"Your trip—are you tired?"

"A little. Even before your call, it was time for me to come. I just wish your grandfather was alive to see the man you have become. He ... we are so proud."

Their heads bowed to each other, talking quietly. Neither noticed Star as she turned into the doorway. Her hand started up to wave, her mouth open to say hello, but stopped. The woman with Ash had to be his grandmother, her gray hair caught in a bun, a black long-sleeve shirt over a black skirt. Star saw the edge of the skirt grace one of her black sturdy shoes against the chair leg.

Star hesitated, hesitant to take another step from the bright hallway into the room with blinds filtering the sunlight. Not wanting to intrude on what was obviously a private moment between grandmother and grandson, she did not enter. Ash's head bent down to his grandmother looking up at him. Her back was straight, no hunching at the shoulders. She was a strong woman speaking in a soft voice.

"Ashar, it is time. You must make a choice. Your life here. A new country, a new community that desperately needs your voice. Or, are you going to return to Syria? You have a passion for speaking the truth, a passionate voice that stirs people to listen. Your grandfather and I tried to give you the opportunity to think for yourself. There are so many misconceptions, painting a picture that all Muslims are bad. But it's a new day ... it can be a new day."

The woman leaned closer, locking eyes with her grandson, forcing him to take in her words.

"Along the way some in the community may break your heart, may turn away, but do not let it break your will. They may not see, may not listen to the truth in your words, that you do not seek or suggest they give up or change their traditions. No, but to understand they can keep the old while embracing the new. They can exist, the traditions, side by side. People fear the unknown.

Fear what is foreign to them. You must use your voice. You must help both sides to be open, to embrace one another, to trust."

There was a rustle at the door as the doctor, white coat flapping, hustled into the room with a nurse, brushing past Star. The doctor had a smile on his face. Star quickly joined in line behind them. "Mr. Rais, your test shows you had a bad bump on your head, and, as you are well aware, a cut."

Ash let his legs fall over the side of bed. Standing, he addressed the man. "Doctor, my grandmother. Grandmother, this nice doctor fixed me up. Oh ... and Star. Star, please, meet my grandmother."

The doctor nodded acknowledging the introduction. Star grasped the grandmother's hand. "So nice to meet you."

She nodded in return with a smile and eyes that seemed to gather Star to her.

"You'll have a headache today, Mr. Rais, but it should clear up by tomorrow. So, Mr. Rais, you are now free to leave. The nurse will give you instructions and paperwork to pick up your personal items that were in your pockets. She told me she already returned your cell phone. If you have any questions give me a call. Anything you want to know now?" The doctor looked at his grandmother, back to Ash.

"No, sir, and thank you." Ash stiffened as a police officer, holstered gun, entered his room.

"Hello, Mr. Rais. I'm Detective Fred Watson. We met but you were a bit groggy at the time. I understand you can leave the hospital, but I'd like you to come with me to the station. We need your statement, for the record, about the robbery and the assault that landed you in the hospital. We also have to talk to you about the status of your student visa. Our records indicate it has expired. Why don't you get dressed. I'll go with you to check out. There is also a matter of paying the hospital for your emergency. Do you have insurance?"

"Yes, he does, Officer." Ash's grandmother stood up. Stood erect. Face stern as she faced the officer. She was not to be trifled with.

"Your name, ma'am?"

"Mrs. Deven Patel, Adhira Patel. I traveled from London ... to help my grandson Ashar. I will accompany him to your station. I have his insurance card with me."

Fred looked from the gray-haired woman to Ash, and back to his grandmother. "I'm sorry, but you'll have to meet us at the station, Mrs. Patel. Here's the address." Watson handed Mrs. Patel his card.

"I'll take you, Mrs. Patel. I just have to make a quick phone call." Star turned to Ash. "You and your grandmother go check out. Mrs. Patel, I'll meet you in the lobby. We can follow Detective Watson." Star slipped out of the room as Ash accepted his clothes from the nurse.

Out in the hall, Star pulled her cell from her purse, and tapped Liz's number.

"Liz, is Manny there? Detective Watson just came to take Ash to the police station. He said he wanted his statement about the robbery and then he said something about his visa being expired."

"Star, we were just on our way to visit Ash. Hang on, I'll put you on speaker. Manny's driving. We'll meet you at the station. Did his grandmother arrive?"

"Yes, she's here. I'm taking her to the station. I think Ash may need your advice ... his visa being expired."

"Of course. Like Liz said, we'll meet you there."

"Manny, he's from Syria, a Muslim. Are they going to deport him?"

"It's possible."

Chapter 34

DETECTIVE WATSON ESCORTED Ashar to the DBPD station, pausing at the bullet-proof lobby window. He paused to tell the duty officer that two women, a Mrs. Patel accompanied by a young woman named Star Bloom would arrive soon. After signing in, he asked the officer to have them escorted to the conference room.

Hearing his name, Watson turned from the duty officer.

"Hey Fred, good to see you." Manny strode up to his friend, hand extended. He smiled at Ash with a quick nod. "Liz and I were just down the hall."

"Manny, Liz, hi ... again. Twice in one day. I thought you were retired." Fred said grasping Manny's hand with a quick pump, then Liz's. "What brings you two here?"

"Well, this man." Manny nodded to Ash a second time, shaking his hand signaling he was there to help. "His friend, Star Bloom, whom you also saw this morning, gave me a call that maybe I could be of some assistance ... to her friend."

"Okay." Fred glanced at the duty officer, then Ash, then out the large plate-glass window. Nothing he could do but to accept the help of his old boss, but he was going to track down how Manny always seemed to show up in the middle of his cases. Maybe the chief didn't trust him with the job. "I see Miss Bloom and Mr. Rais's grandmother getting out of a van ... Charlie's Diner." Fred glanced at Ash. "Come on, Mr. Rais. Let's go to the conference room. They'll catch up."

Entering the windowless room with a long oak table in the center, chairs tucked under, Fred nodded to Ash. "Take any seat, Mr. Rais. Would you like a cup of coffee, glass of water?"

"N-n-no, thank you, sir."

With a soft knock, the door swung open and Star, holding Mrs. Patel's arm, stepped into the conference room. Mrs. Patel, her eyes sweeping the room, took a seat next to Ashar, patting his hand, whispering to him not to worry.

"Thanks, Manny, Liz, for coming," Star said in a soft voice taking a seat on the other side of Ash.

"No problem. Glad to help if I can," Manny said.

Liz, sitting beside Manny, leaned back in the black metal folding chair, took a deep breath, releasing the air in a silent sigh. This was her husband's territory, his old stomping ground. Retired or not, at one time the Captain of the Criminal Investigation Division, DBPD-CID, he was still respected by the force, still called upon for help. It rarely happened that she accompanied him in DBPD's hallowed halls. In such instances, they had made an agreement that he would always take the lead, she would observe. If she spotted something, good or bad, she'd note it on a pad of paper, slide it into his view.

Today was such an instance. She looked blankly around the room, withdrawing a yellow pad from her shoulder bag as Detective Watson began the meeting.

"Mr. Rais, please tell me, for the record, what you saw, what you did, and how you received a blow on the head that landed you in the hospital." Fred, flipped on the recorder lying in the center of the table between him and Ash. Fred nodded for Ash to go ahead.

"I-I-I was waiting for Star. The diner was closing ... no one left ... when a man with a sweater came in asking for coffee. Tyler ... the waiter ... told the man there wasn't any. T-T-Told him to come back in the morning. Then everything happened fast. Star came out, the man grabbed her, pulled a gun, pointed it at her, and I took him out. The man swung at me ... no, that's not right. The man held the gun to Star's head, demanded money. Tyler took bills from the register, shoved them at the man. The man yelled to get the rest ... of the money. That's when I took him out b-b-but he took me out. I guess I hit my head on the counter as I went down. That's all I know. I w-w-woke up in the hospital."

Fred stopped the recorder. "Excuse me, everyone, while I have this typed up. Take a break. There's coffee, water on the table by the door. Help yourself. I won't be long."

"Mrs. Patel, can I get you something to drink?" Star asked looking around Ash to his grandmother.

"Do you suppose I could have a cup of tea, dear?"

Liz stood, stretched, raised her eyes to Manny. "Sure, Come on, Star. I'll help you find a teabag ... some hot water."

"Ask the duty officer, front desk. She'll fix it for you. Sugar, milk?" Manny asked Mrs. Patel.

Shaking her head, Liz grasped Star's arm, leading her out of the room.

"Liz, what do you think? What's really going on?" Star asked.

"Not sure, except I think Detective Watson is just warming up."

A few minutes later, Fred returned followed by Star and Liz. Star set a teacup, teabag on the side, in front of Mrs. Patel and returned to her seat on the other side of Ash. Liz, locking eyes with Manny for an instant, returned to her seat beside him.

"Okay, Mr. Rais, here's a copy of your statement, what you saw take place at the diner Monday night. Please read it and, if it's accurate, sign at the bottom that you have read the report and you agree with it. If there are any changes or additional information you want to include just let me know." Noting Mrs. Patel had a cup of tea, he asked if Star or Liz would like coffee. Both women shook their heads watching Ash sign the one-page report, sliding it to the Detective sitting across the table.

"Thank you, Mr. Rais. Now, it is a standard practice, when a victim of an assault is hospitalized in our jurisdiction, for the hospital to send a report to us, Daytona Beach Police Department. This practice gives us the information we need to help in the apprehension of the person who perpetrated the assault. In this case, the robber, the person who struck you ending in your head injury."

"Have you found him already?" Star leaned forward, her hands grasping the edge of the oak conference table.

"Not yet, Miss Bloom. Now, Mr. Rais, further, as a routine matter, when a name is sent to us, for whatever reason, that name is automatically scanned through the Florida Investigation database in Tallahassee. Sometimes the name pops up as a match for someone we are looking for, or, as a matter of record, has committed some crime in the past. Such is the case of your name, Ashar Rais."

"B-B-but I've never been arrested. I've never committed a r-r-robbery."

"No, we didn't find that you had committed a felony. But, I'm afraid we did find that you are in this country illegally. Your visa expired a month ago."

"Detective, that was my fault. Mr. Patel, Ashar's grandfather, was going to process the paperwork but unfortunately, it was delayed ... due to his death."

"I'm sorry for your loss, Mrs. Patel, but no matter who's at fault, the visa was not renewed, and your grandson will have to leave the United States in the next few days."

"I think not, Detective. You see my husband and I were having serious discussions, long distance telephone conversations, with our grandson, on whether Ashar should remain in the U.S. Ashar felt a responsibility to his family but very much wanted to stay in the United States. A country he had grown to respect. My husband and I agreed that he should remain in Florida."

"But Mrs. Patel, he can't just *decide* to stay. There is a process. I'm afraid he will have to return with you, or to ... let me see, yes, return to Damascus, Syria, according to his visa, his country of origin, or London with you. He just can't stay here. Then, he can apply to Immigration to start the process to come to the U.S. legally."

"I understand what you're saying, Detective Watson. But ... Ashar, I'm sorry you have to learn of what I'm about to say in this manner. Please forgive the deception your mother and I held since your birth." Mrs. Patel patted his hand, worry lines deepening around her eyes. She opened her purse retrieving a worn, dog-eared envelope. "You see, Detective, my grandson is already a citizen of the United States. He was born in New York, Calvary Hospital in the Bronx."

"Grandmother?" Ash jumped to his feet. Looked down at his grandmother. "This can't be true."

Mrs. Patel grasped her grandson's forearm. "Yes, Ashar, it is true. Your mother and I traveled to the United States under the pretense of seeing a sick friend. She was eight months pregnant but your father thought she was only six months along ... easy to hide under her heavy clothing. We had a plan. We did not want her baby to follow in your father's or your brother's footsteps. Footsteps that seemed to take them further and further into the militant ways of those around them. So we came to the United States purposely to see that you were born here."

Mrs. Patel did not turn away from her grandson. Did not look at the detective. Others heard what she was saying, but her words were for Ashar.

"Within four days after your birth, we traveled to India, to Kapas Hera, a village where I was permitted to attend school as a young woman and where I met your grandfather. Your mother and I told people that you were born in a little inn with the help of a midwife. No papers, just a beautiful baby boy. Your mother called your father, told him that she had the baby before she could join him in Damascus, told him she would return to him as soon as she could travel."

"But grandmother, I have papers showing I was born in Syria, in Damascus."

"Yes, your father went to the government offices, told them of the circumstances of your birth in Kapas Hera, and under those conditions requested the official give him papers, a certificate of birth proving his son, Ashar Rais, was a Syrian citizen. How you ask? He knew the right people, the right official who did this for him ... for you. After all, your father was a trusted member of the military. A man who could be counted on—when he was ordered to do something he did it. Willingly."

"D-D-did my father know of this deception?"

"Never. No one knows this—only your mother knew and I. And now you know the truth."

"I guess that does it, Fred," Manny said. "He's an American citizen. I know you'll track this down in the Bronx, visit the hospital, verify the birth certificate just to be sure."

"That I will, Manny. That I will. But, Mr. Rais, I urge you to stay in Florida, or let us know if you plan to travel, until I can verify that this birth certificate is authentic."

Fred looked down at the folder lying on the table in front of him. He grunted, a shallow sigh, looked across the table at Ash. "However, there is another matter, Mr. Rais. Seems your family name, Rais, turned up in a Homeland Security alert. The name is linked to potential terrorist activity, activity targeting the U.S."

Chapter 35

THERE IT WAS, the next shoe dropping with a thud that reverberated off the walls of the stark conference room. Rais now equated with terrorist.

Manny waited.

He saw Ash's eyes snap up in shock, then fear. His family's name had made it onto the United States Homeland Security terrorist list—a terrorist watch list.

Mrs. Patel's eyes darted to her grandson. She understood that the detective's revelation could mean years of trouble for Ashar and she was going to do her best to show that, while he might carry the name of a terrorist, Ashar did not have a radical bone in his body. She knew that his father had died a few months earlier in a raid, his brother escaping. One Rais down, leaving one more to cause trouble. She had told Ashar of his father's death and warned him to be wary of his brother.

She also knew that the new head of the Rais family wanted Ashar to come home to Syria, wanted him to join the fight against the west. Something Ashar would never do.

"Has your brother told you he is coming to the U.S. to visit you, Mr. Rais?" The pen between Fred's fingers twitched, tapping the pad of yellow paper lying on the table in front of him, waiting for the answer.

"W-W-we haven't spoken for two years."

"Your mother, then?"

"She was killed. I saw her die. I held her—her final breath."

"I have something for you, Mr. Rais." The detective nodded to Manny. "Mr. Salinas found your gold chain ... and the ring ... at a pawn shop."

Watson reached in his pocket, laid the chain and ring on Ashar's outstretched palm. Tears welled in his eyes, remembering his mother, remembered her whispering to take the ring from her finger as she lay dying in his arms, a ring to remember her by.

Ash in turn laid the ring on his grandmother's palm. Stifling a gasp, she pressed it to her lips. "My baby girl."

Ashar fumbled with the clasp on the chain. Star quickly stood, stepped behind him, fastening the chain around his neck.

"Now, Mr. Rais, your brother." Detective Watson continued.

Mrs. Patel, with a deep sigh, tapped the nail of her finger on the table, affording her another second to regain her composure. "Ashar is estranged from his family, Detective Watson, and has been ever since he came to London to live with his grandfather and me. You, Detective Watson, must guard against lumping all Muslims together, the good with the bad. Ever since September eleven, two thousand and one, that horrific day, the date you term 9/11, has defined all Muslims as terrorists. I was visiting friends in New York City that day. My close friend lost her brother in the North Tower."

Star, her breathing ragged, listened to Ash's story unfold, the story about what he had gone through, the past that made the man what he is today. He had never confided in her. Yes, she had wondered, but never pressed for answers. She had babbled on about her life and now realized he told her virtually nothing about his. What horrors had he seen? His mother dying in his arms?

"As the horrific scenes streamed from my friend's television throughout that day and night, and those that followed, the unfathomable story unfolded of the radical middle-east men who flew those planes." Mrs. Patel closed her eyes, breathing deep, seeing her friend. Opening her eyes, she continued. "Believe me when I say those terrorists do not reflect the religion they rely on to justify their cause. They wrecked the lives of people like my friends who had come to America to live a free, safe life. Those men do not believe in Allah, our God, or your God.

"My friends and I began to realize what this might mean for us Muslims. Within hours when we ventured outside, as all Americans did, gathering in the streets, tears rolling down our cheeks, we were stared at, curses hurled at us as if we were responsible for this sin. We kept our heads down, but we could see the merchants in the neighborhood, Muslim merchants quickly display the American flag showing their solidarity with their country, America. But non-Muslim citizens turned on the merchants, threw stones through their shop windows—bakeries, shoe stores, butcher shops—a few hours earlier, those same shopkeepers thought of their neighbors as friends.

"My husband, Ashar's grandfather, pleaded with me to return to London, warning me that I wasn't safe in America. Not safe in America? I had done nothing wrong. Fear ran through the neighborhood—fear of being rounded up into internment camps as had been the case in World War II with some Japanese and Germans who were American Citizens.

"Planes were grounded for two days. Then some airlines began to fly under strict security. I was able to change my return ticket from November third to September eighteenth, seven days after this attack on your homeland.

"During the days following, while I waited to catch my flight, the women on our block did not wear veils, wearing instead jeans, T-shirts, anything Western, hoping they would not be targeted. The men shaved their beards, clipped their hair. Names were changed—Ali became Alan, Salim, my friend's husband, chose to be known as Sam.

"We heard stories of citizens taking advantage of the situation, turning on their own—a robbery of a convenience store owned by a Christian, a Rabbi robbed at knifepoint. It seemed no one was safe."

Star sat mute, stunned by Mrs. Patel's words. Had she shown fear when she visited the still smoking ruins, the ash-covered sidewalks. When she saw a veiled woman, had she made a hateful face? Had she feared them?

The conference room filled with silence, silence filled with memories of that day—where they were when they heard a plane had struck a building in New York City. Remembered the horror as the minutes, hours, days unfolded. Now, here was another victim's story. The story of Mrs. Patel and her friend.

Mrs. Patel stared at the group around the table, but she didn't see them. The images in her mind were back with her friends, and the tears shed following the aftermath of nine-eleven. In hushed tones she rambled on. "We felt great guilt for something we didn't do. When I returned to London, my husband and I wondered how we could protect our grandson. Foolish thoughts because Ashar was becoming a man, a man who would choose his own path.

"As a youngster Ashar feared guns, shrank out of sight when his father and brother left the house during the night heavily armed. Ashar saw unspeakable horrors. He began to stutter when confronted with authority, authority that could easily cut out his tongue if he said something they didn't agree with. His father didn't understand the boy, seeing weakness instead of revulsion for what his father stood for."

Star sat, staring down at her folded hands resting on the table. Her thoughts swirling with what she had just heard. Ash had magnetism about him. She could see him being a spokesman for the community because he spoke from the heart. So what was Mrs. Patel really saying? That Ash was groomed for a life she and his grandfather saw for him? Is that a life Ash really wants to live? Is this why he seemed reticent to reach out to her?

Chapter 36

THERE WAS NO CHATTER, no glib remarks, no smiles as everyone filed out of the conference room.

The revelations over the last hour hit Ash hard. He had never been told the details of his birth, about the deception. While stunning to learn he was born in the United States, a citizen by birth, it did not alter his path, did not change his mission in life. He realized the burden of the deception that his grandmother had born was a heavy one, weighing on her shoulders all these years. He also knew the revelations were a shock to Star.

They had to talk.

Detective Watson said goodbye as the group assembled outside the Daytona Beach Police Department building. He reminded Ashar to keep him apprised of his whereabouts if he traveled outside Volusia County. The detective would notify Mr. Rais once his birth certificate was authenticated, as well as any further issues having to do with his brother.

Standing outside in the late afternoon heat, Liz whispered to Manny, his head bent down to her. Nodding, he turned to Mrs. Patel. "How long are you staying, Mrs. Patel?"

"I'm returning to London tomorrow ... early, from Daytona Beach Airport. There are many connections."

"You'll stay with me, Grandmother. I'll have an extra bed brought to my room." Ash looked at Manny. "My car is at The Crescent Moon, my motel on the beach." He shook his head. "An ambulance, the detective ... I've had rides of one kind or another since the robbery. Can I ask you to take my grandmother and me—"

"Not a problem, Ash," Manny said laying his hand on Ash's shoulder. He looked at Liz, gazed around the group. "Liz and I thought maybe everyone would like to relax, let's say decompress. We'd like to take you all to dinner. There's a casual restaurant on the Daytona Beach pier—The Crab Shack." Seeing a hint of smile on Mrs. Patel's face, Manny plunged on. "Yes, Mrs. Patel, a touch of Florida. We'll drive. Star, I see you have the diner's van."

"I really should return it. The diner isn't far from the pier. Ash, do you want to come with me ... we'll catch up with the others?"

Nodding, he hugged his grandmother, walked alongside Star to the van. Manny helped Mrs. Patel up onto the front seat of his black SUV as Liz scooted into the backseat.

Climbing into the van, Star kept breathing deep, her fingers shaking as she tried to insert the car keys into the ignition. There was so much she wanted to say. So much she wanted to ask. But she didn't know how to start ... where to start.

The drive to the diner, only minutes away, was nerve racking.

Ash leaned his head back, arm up holding onto the roll bar. "The pier ... can we talk?"

"Yes, yes. That's good." Star's eyes remained trained on the road.

Chapter 37

LIZ CALLED AHEAD to the Crab Shack, asked the woman answering to please save a table by a window, a table for five, a good table for a guest from London. Manny smiled looking at his wife in the rearview mirror. Of course, a window table would be more than nice. He had promised Liz if she had to give up something during her pregnancy he would give it up too, such as alcohol. But he hoped she'd give him a pass this one time. He really wanted a martini.

Picking up the lack of conversation, Liz leaned over from the backseat, describing to Mrs. Patel the points of interest. Manny noticed that Mrs. Patel seemed content to let the perky redhead jabber away.

Within short order the traumatized group reunited at a window table. Mrs. Patel with a glass of sparkling water, Star, Ash and Liz holding glasses of iced tea and lemon, Manny an extra large martini—three olives.

Over dinner, the conversation quiet at first, reserved, turned to Liz and Manny's pending event. The mood around the table lightened and Ash, picking up Star's hand, suggested they take a walk along the pier. Excusing themselves, they walked to the back of the restaurant, stepping out into the somewhat cooler air overlooking the ocean.

Ash stuffed his hands in his pants pockets. Liz wrapped her arms around herself as if she were cold but really trying to hold herself together. He kept his eyes straight ahead. He had to tell Star he was leaving, leaving her. His feelings for her had begun to swamp his thoughts. He knew she had dreams of her own, very different than his. He also knew they had no future.

"I like your grandmother. She's devoted to you."

"She's been through a lot ... seen a lot."

"The way she talks about your grandfather, their plans for you ... are they your plans too?"

Ash looked out over the ocean, down at the waves lapping at the pilings, the pier's foundation. He leaned against the weathered railing, Star standing close to his side.

"Their plans are mine. My passion, my dream is to be my community's voice in America, to tell Americans that it wasn't the Muslim community, a God worshiping, respectful people desiring peace, freedom to pray in their own way ... no, it wasn't the peace-loving Muslims they should fear, but the radical, militant Islamists. I believe in my destiny, I believe I was born to be a voice for my community.

"My grandmother's passion and my passion, coupled with my training in Media Communications, have given me the voice to reach out to other Muslims across the United States, to show them how to get their message out, their message that they love America and would never harm her. Quite the opposite, they want to protect her and the freedoms she offers."

Ash looked at Star, his eyes scanning her face. Did she understand what he was trying to tell her?

"Our cultures seem to clash but they don't need to. There are so many similarities ... such as the belief in one God. Dreams to live a full rich life. A life of peace, respect for our elders, respect for one another. But this message is not heard. Young Muslims are torn between the past, the traditions of their parents, and how they wish to live in the present and the future. Many are confused. The older generation fears their traditions, their values are being lost. I wish my voice to reach the old as well as the young, that neither should fear this new world of freedom.

"What is so sad, is that great progress was being made. Then nine-eleven trashed it for all of us. It seems both sides view each other as an oddity, failing to understand how much each shares with the other. All need to reflect and then move forward to a brighter future.

"Please excuse my ramblings. I feel deeply about my mission, my choice to be a voice."

"You're so young to speak with such passion and when you speak with passion you don't stutter. Why is that?" Star asked.

Ashar was exhausted—his head wound, his grandmother by his side once again, from the enormity of the task ahead of him. He turned to Star, slowly wrapping her in his arms, she weaving her hands around his neck, nestling against his chest.

Releasing her, he inched back, his eyes grazing her hair, her lips, her eyes. "You are a beautiful woman, Star. Yes, you are beautiful outside but you have beauty inside as well. From the moment I first walked into the diner—"

"You were looking for a job—"

"Yes. We joked about applying to be a cook. Remember?"

She nodded, her eyes searching his face.

Closing his eyes, Ash again wrapped his arms around her, whispering, releasing the words caught in a stranglehold within his throat. "I'm leaving for Miami. There's a community of Muslims in Miami who fled the persecution in Cuba, who came to America. I'll stay a few months ... then Michigan, probably Detroit. No one noticed, but I hung back as everyone walked to the cars. I told Detective Watson my plans and that I would keep him informed as to my whereabouts."

"But you have a job. You're a reporter ... your paper, the requirement for your degree."

"I met with my professor giving him my final paper the day before ... the day before the robbery. I submitted the story to the News Journal for the latest assignment the same day."

"But, but they wanted you for the summer, and, and you said they promised there would be more assignments after that. My bakeoff competition—another week. I promised Wanda and

Charlie I'd stay through the summer—only a few more weeks. We—"

Ash put his finger to her lips, stopping her from saying more. "Maybe if we had met at a different time ... our lives might have taken a different path." He touched her hair, moved a strand that had fallen across her cheek. "The day I walked into the diner, saw your innocent blue eyes, the gold waves of your hair ... I wish you well. You're strong. Bring your dreams to life, Star Bloom. I ... I must go."

"When?" Air stuck in her throat, her body limp, she reached out grasping his arm, disbelief falling over her face, filling her eyes, mouth open to speak but no words could express the hurt. Fearing his words, steeling herself, knowing in her heart what he was going to say ...

"Tomorrow."

"Tomorrow?" she whispered shaking her head, gulping for air, swiping at a tear.

Taking her hand, he led her back to the others.

They were standing, ready to leave.

Manny and Liz hugged Mrs. Patel, wishing her a safe journey back to London and shook Ash's hand. Manny told him to call if he needed any further assistance.

Ash dropped Star's hand as his grandmother kissed her on the cheek. "God speed, my dear."

Ash steadied his grandmother, threading her arm through his, holding her hand in a strong grip. They walked out of the restaurant, down the pier to the street, steps slow at first, then gaining in stride.

Star watched as he walked away from her.

Liz could feel her friend's distress. She jerked her head at Manny. They had to do something to help her.

Liz stepped to Star's left, took her hand as Manny stepped to her other side draping his arm around her shoulders.

"He's leaving ... for good," Star whispered.

Liz squeezed Star's hand. "How about we take a walk on the beach?"

Star nodded.

Removing his arm from her shoulder, Manny held the glass door open for his wife as she led Star out onto the old wooden pier, to the steps down to the beach. Ash and Mrs. Patel were out of sight.

A soft breeze cooled the humid air. A couple strolled barefoot, hand in hand at the edge of the surf, their three children squealing as a small wave rolled over their toes.

Star glanced up at the Bandshell. A stage crew was preparing for a concert. People were laughing, laying blankets on the sand, staking out their spot on the beach.

Star dropped Liz's hand folding her arms across her chest. "Ash is a good person ... don't you think?"

Manny, his hands at his side as he moseyed along. "Yes, he is, Star. He's wise beyond his years."

Liz stooped to pick up a shell. "I can't imagine what it must have been like, his mother dying in his arms."

"Do you think he's doing what he really wants to do, a missionary of sorts, I guess. Or is it because he feels an obligation to his grandparents?" Star asked.

"Either way ... it doesn't matter," Manny said. "He's not a boy—his past, the people close to him, have had an influence, but in the end he settled on the path he wanted to pursue."

Liz gazed out over the sparkling waves. "He seems to have the conviction to follow ... what did he say ... his destiny? It's not often we meet someone with such strength."

"So, I guess I'm fortunate that our lives touched this summer. I'll never forget him."

"You're strong, Star. You keep moving forward. You don't let anyone beat you down."

"But my goals aren't as lofty as his."

"Whoa. Think of the people, hundreds I dare say, you brought joy to this summer. You have a talent with the mainstay of human existence—food. Remember how the diner was dying until you came along. And now look—it's standing room only. And the kids, the parents, everyone's flocking to the diner because of you." Liz grabbed Star's hand, swinging her arm up in triumph.

"... and Ty. You can't leave him out of the diner's success."

"Oh, that young man has such a big heart."

Manny smiled at the two women. "You know, Star, when you think about it, the three of you, Ash, Tyler, and yourself touched each other's lives this summer heading in three very different directions. Yes, I'd say the three of you are lucky to have had such an experience. Don't you, Stitch?"

"Absolutely. And that, dear husband, is what our friend must do—look to the future. When's the next bakeoff, Star?"

"Tomorrow."

"Well, you put a smile on that face, throw those shoulders back, and kick ass."

Star laughed.

"What's funny?" Liz asked. "I was trying to be uplifting."

"Ty said those exact words a couple of days ago."

"What did I say—that boy's smart."

"You said he had heart."

Liz giggled, snuggling against Star's arm. "Well, that too."

Chapter 38

FRIDAY

READY WITH STAR'S large coffee, high test, black, Tyler nervously tapped the steering wheel waiting for her to step out the door of her apartment. He was going to do his level best to pump up her adrenalin for today's competition. He was driving his mom's Lincoln. She told him to borrow her car whenever Star was due at the bakeoff, no matter the day. Tyler offered to swap with his Harley, but Cindy only laughed—she wanted to live a little longer.

When Star emerged a minute later, his lips turned down in a grimace. "Uh oh, my Kewpie doll doesn't look happy." Jumping out, he held the car door, nodded to her greeting—a very weak, "Hi."

Back behind the wheel, he accelerated up the street, turned south on Atlantic Avenue, turning west on International Speedway.

He stole a quick glance as she heaved a sigh, ventured a sip of coffee. Yup, something's up. "Are you okay?"

Star nodded.

"Well, you should tell your face you're okay, because—"

"Ash is gone." Another sip of coffee, blank stare out the window.

"Gone, like gone gone, or gone like gone fishing?"

"Miami. A few months, then Michigan ... probably Detroit."

"He said that?"

"Word for word."

"Gee, kinda sudden."

"Oh, there's more ... later."

"Yeah, right. Well, here we are. Break a leg ... no, I don't mean that. Good luck. As before, I'll be back at six unless you text me ... text me anytime ... you know, if you want to chat."

"Thanks, Ty. Have a good day."

He watched as she walked to the entrance, joined by another baker grasping the handle of a rolling suitcase, a foam cup of coffee in hand.

• • •

"GREETINGS, BAKERS."

Jim Whisk and Stephanie Hall, standing side by side, beamed back at the contestants. "I hope you enjoyed your day off. As you can see, we're down to six. Two bakers withdrew after you left on Wednesday. Steph and I huddled and we decided on another change in the schedule, which, I think you will agree, will make for a dramatic finish, one that will keep the audience out in television land screaming to find out the winner."

Jim paused, looked from face to face. What did he expect—applause?

"Don't forget, ask your family and friends to come to the celebration tomorrow. They're invited for the entire bakeoff, refreshments to follow."

He didn't know about the bakers, but he was excited. It would be a great final episode. A potential cliffhanger.

"As before, you will present your final product to the judges." Jim and Steph turned to the two celebrity chefs who were exchanging quizzical looks—another schedule change?

"Today will be the semifinal round with a double elimination—that's right, two of you will be sent home today."

The bakers looked at each other, groaning. Double elimination.

Seemingly oblivious to the contestants' angst, Jim continued on. Upbeat. "The big finish, the finals, the crowning of the winner of the Amateur Baking Competition, will be tomorrow. We won't keep you on pins and needles for days and days. Tomorrow you will know which one of you wins the prize."

Jim and Steph smiled, swapped glances. This time his announcement of the changes was received to applause from the competitors. Received way better than they dared hoped for.

"Now, let's go over why we're here—the baking. Today there will be two categories—*bread* and *cookies*. You will choose two of your personal favorites for each category. Two different loaves of bread. Two kinds of cookies, a dozen each. The savory offerings everyone in your circle of family and friends keep asking you to bake. You will have two and a half hours to bake your loaves of bread. Remember, choose your favorites. Your best. When time is called set your product at the end of your counter returning to the center of your work station. There will be a forty-five minute break between *bread* and *cookies*.

"Today, instead of presenting the baked item to the judges they will come to you. The judges will step to your counter to rank your efforts by presentation and taste. As I said before, at the end of the day, two of you will be sent home. The remaining four competitors will return tomorrow when one of you will be crowned the winner of the Amateur Bakeoff Competition."

Satisfied with his remarks, pleased that everyone took the changes in stride, Jim set them loose.

"Bakers, the category is *bread*. Let the baking begin."

Activity burst throughout the hall—clanging pans, tapping of glass bowls and banging of cupboard doors and utensil drawers.

Star flipped through Gran's treasured recipes in the little metal recipe binder to the tab labeled bread. She found the two breads that she and Gran had baked almost every Thanksgiving—Zucchini, and a rich Greek olive and cheese. Fearing the producers hadn't stocked the produce section with what she needed, she ran to the shelves, bins, and cabinets in the rear of the hall. Her fears were quickly allayed. The zucchinis were small, fresh, perfect. She snatched them before another baker had a chance. She had learned from the previous episodes to decide quickly on what she needed, visiting the produce, and condiment section from the shelves before anyone else.

She returned to her station after picking out the zucchini, and what she needed for the olive and cheese loaf. If only she made it through today, she'd be in the finals tomorrow.

As time whizzed by, the hall filled with the mouth-watering scents of baking bread.

The loaves of bread were inspected, tasted by the judges. The decision was made.

Star came in first.

During her break she called Gran with the new schedule. If she wasn't eliminated today, she'd be in the finals now scheduled for tomorrow. They had a brief conversation about cookies. Star picked out two that she and Gran baked every Christmas for the family, and had filled small tins as gifts for friends—no-bake chocolate and coconut drops, bourbon-almond balls rolled in powdered sugar. Gran agreed with her selections and wished her luck.

Soon the rich aroma of cookie dough permeated the air, circling around the bakers, the judges, and Jim and Stephanie.

At first Star was sure she wouldn't finish in time, then again she felt she was okay, only to realize she had missed a step. She quickly tried to recover the time.

Suddenly Jim called out, "Five minutes, bakers."

"Two minutes, bakers."

"One minute, bakers. Put your cookie platters at the end of your counter."

Somehow she had managed to block from her mind everything that happened the day before—Ash, his grandmother, all of the secrets, the agonies, and the words running and rerunning—*when are you leaving?—tomorrow!*

The judges again made the rounds to each baker, sampling, judging, commenting. Jim, Stephanie, and the judges huddled.

Jim picked up the microphone. First, he gave the names of the bakers who were sent home. A young girl was one—she was so stressed during the competition she burned one loaf of bread, and most of her cookies.

Then, not wasting any time, he announced the cookie winner.

Star came in second.

She was in the finals.

So, the finalists numbered four.

One of the remaining bakers had suffered burns on her hand while removing a sheet of cookies from the oven. The baker said she didn't care if she had to bake with one hand, she'd be back tomorrow.

The day's competition was over.

Star barely had enough energy to put Gran's recipe book in her duffel bag. Jim hadn't said what the category would be for the finals, but if she had to bet, she'd bet it would be baker's choice.

Her choice—Gran's taffy.

Taking one last inventory of the supply shelves she stumbled out to the car. Ty gallantly held the car door for her.

Tyler didn't talk.

Star didn't talk, dozing off the minute she laid back against the headrest.

Chapter 39

EVERYONE HAD LEFT—the bakers and the cameramen.

Jim sipped a beer. Stephanie uncapped an icy bottle of water. They sat on scratched gray-metal folding chairs in the back office going over the remaining hours of the competition.

"Today went well, don't you think, Steph?"

"We were lucky, Jim. I spoke to the owner of the building. Told him we would vacate by six o'clock tomorrow night. I asked him to meet us, check out the premises, and return our damage deposit."

"You were so smart to write in an escape clause, Steph. Thank heavens, no further requirement for the space. What about the rental company? All the stations—refrigerators, ovens?"

"Five o'clock tomorrow afternoon the truck will roll in—pack up and roll out. I didn't say anything to the cameramen, but they obviously know their gig will end because of your announcement—the competition finals. They may assume we would like additional shots. A wrong assumption. They will hand over the flash drives with the files, all the episodes, and we give them the final check."

They sighed in unison. Jim took another sip of beer.

Stephanie took a swig from her bottled water.

"I do have some good news, excellent news," Stephanie said recapping her bottle. "The Orlando cable news network, actually, there are three that accepted my invitation to be on hand tomorrow—film background during the day and interview the winner at the end. Also the local paper, The News Journal, is sending a reporter along with a cameraman. But the really, really big news ... "

"Yes? The really big news is?"

"Our agent emailed me that maybe we'll have a contract to sign after all, as in tomorrow. A contract for *syndication* of the Florida Amateur Baker Competition Series."

Jim jumped up, threw his hands in the air, crossed his hands behind his neck, looked at the ceiling, shut his eyes. "Oh my God ... syndication!"

Chapter 40

TYLER TURNED DOWN Star's street and pulled to the curb. "Well, who do we have here?" He nudged Star with his elbow. "Star, wake up. Of course, I could be mistaken, but from what you've said about her, I think your grandmother is standing at your front door."

"What?" Star stretched, yawned, rubbed her eyes. "My grandmother? GRAN?"

Star screamed, jumped from the car, ran to her Gran's open arms.

"Gran, Gran, you don't know how happy I am to see you. But we talked earlier. How did you get here so fast?"

"Cell phones are wonderful. You didn't know but I was already on my way. I was about to board a plane."

Tyler stood back, holding her duffle bag, shifting from foot to foot.

Gran saw the man standing by the car, looking a bit uncertain as to whether he should join them or ...

"Star dear, the young man—"

"Oh, yes ... Tyler, come here. Meet my Gran. Gran this is Tyler Jackman—my lifesaver.

"Hello, Tyler. Star talks about you all the time. I believe you are Star's cherry lifesaver. Me, maybe lemon. A little tart." Gran laughed encasing him in a warm hug.

Not knowing what he should do with his arms, Tyler hugged her back. "Are you two hungry? I can take you out or—"

"Ty, could you run up to the corner, get a pizza, then join us for dinner. I'm sure Gran's tired and I can barely move."

"Sure, sure. Thanks. I'd like that. Back in a flash. But I won't stay. You two have a lot to catch up on ... and planning for the finals. I believe you said something about your Gran's taffy," he said with a broad smile.

Gran hugged him again.

Star stood with tears streaming down her face ... Gran was with her. "My support team," she managed to say giving Ty a hug.

"Well, maybe I can stay for a couple of slices."

Chapter 41

TYLER POKED HIS HEAD in the kitchen, said hi to his mom and dad, scratched Cleo behind the ears. "One more day, Mom. The final bakeoff is tomorrow and Star's still in the running. Took a first and a second today."

Cindy clapped her hands. "That's wonderful, isn't it, Tony."

"It sure is. Will it be all right if your mom and I come to watch the finals?"

"What do you think, Tyler? But, we wouldn't want to impose."

"I think she'd love you both to be there. Guess what."

"What, dear?"

"Her grandmother flew in today from Hoboken. Can you believe it? You should have heard the two of them—chattering like magpies. Two minutes earlier Star was asleep in the car as I drove her home. Then, there she was standing at her front door. We all had pizza. It was a riot. She's a very nice lady. You'll like her, and I think she'd like to sit with you. Anyway, I'll ask Star in the morning when would be a good time. My guess is, when I pick up Star in the morning, I pick up her grandmother, too. She'll probably be there all day."

"Your mom and I were just having a glass of wine," Tony said topping off their glasses. "Would you like a glass?"

"Nah, thanks. I have an open bottle upstairs."

"Cindy, how about we take everyone to dinner after the competition—win, lose, or draw?"

"Tony, that's a wonderful idea. Star will be tired, so nothing too fancy. Tyler, text me with whatever Star would like?"

"I will, Mom. Thanks again for the use of the car—one more day. I'm heading up. See you when I see you ... tomorrow. I'll text."

"You have some mail, dear. I put it by your computer."

"Thanks, Mom."

Tyler kissed his mom, hugged his dad, and ambled up to his studio.

Hitting three buttons on the panel by the door—the indirect lighting came on, the ceiling fan began to stir the air, and the AC clicked in. Tyler noted it wasn't very hot ... his mom had turned down the AC anticipating his arrival. He poured a glass of wine, unlaced his sneakers, kicking them off under the table, picked up the mail and settled in his lounger.

He flicked through the envelopes, flyers, registration return card for his new 3-D printer, and a letter from California.

A LETTER POSTMARKED BURBANK CALIFORNIA!!

Tyler jumped up, slit the envelope, and read the enclosed letter.

Dear Mr. Tyler Jackman,

We will be sending you an email early next week with the particulars of our offer, an offer to join us on a project we have just signed with DreamWorks.

Our firm will act as a subcontractor on a new feature animated film.

We were very impressed with your submission: The Little Baker Girl. In fact, we'd like to discuss developing the story into a short film.

If possible, can you join us by September 1. We will pay for your travel and living expenses for the first three months, along with a salary. All of this will be explained in the email.

We look forward to hearing from you after you receive this letter and the following email. Hopefully you will accept our offer. If your answer is yes, you will receive a check to cover your relocation expenses. In the meantime, please call with any questions. I'm sure you have some.

Sincerely,
Thomas Dodd
Production Coordinator

"Mom! Dad! Mom, Mom, Dad," Tyler yelled, scrambling out of his studio, down the circular staircase, through the dining room, into the kitchen.

"Look at this. Read. Read. Do you think it's real?"

His dad reached for the letter his son was waving at him. Snaring it from his fingers, he and Cindy, heads together, read the letter. Looking at each other then turning to Tyler, the three did a group hug after Tyler finally stopped jumping up and down.

Chapter 42

SATURDAY

GRINNING, A GRIN THAT wouldn't stop, Tyler pulled to the curb in front of Star's building. Hopping out of the car, he raced to the door, hand raised to knock as the door swung open. Chattering, Star and Gran stepped out into the brilliant morning sunshine. Hugging Tyler, the pair continued walking to the car, Star pulling a large roll-along case. The topic—what categories would the producers pick for the bakeoff finals, and what recipes Star should choose?

Laughing, Tyler jogged to the car, relieved Star of the case and opened the back door. The women definitely needed to sit side by side to solve the issue of their intense discussion.

Stashing the case in the trunk, climbing behind the wheel, adjusting the mirror, his lips stretched to the limit at his passengers. "Your chauffer, my ladies. We shall be at the arena in precisely twelve minutes."

"Thanks, Ty. Gran, there are only two categories left ... plus, the final round. I'd bet my life that they will leave the last round up to us bakers. So, your taffy it will be."

"Did you bring the apothecary jars, dear? You know how pretty the various colors look on display."

"Yes, five. Five colors—lime, lemon, orange, peach, and red and white stripe peppermint."

"Beautiful. Tyler, how are you this morning, dear?"

"Couldn't be better, Madame. You look well, roses on your cheeks."

"Oh, Tyler, you are something else. While I'm here, you have to show me your cartoons. Star has raved about them all summer."

"Happy to, my lady. But first, we must deposit the damsel at the competition. Mademoiselle, here is my handkerchief. Put it in your apron pocket for luck." Tyler kissed the white linen square, handing it over his head with a wave to Star in the backseat.

"Thanks, Ty." With a giggle, Star stuffed the handkerchief down the neck of her fresh white blouse.

"Ah, a little laugh, my lady. Your heart is a bit lighter today, I think."

"You look like an adorable baker doll, Star," Gran said. "White blouse, short black skirt, black shoes. The frilly apron is perfect. Is this the uniform for all the contestants?"

"No. We choose our outfits. As the producer said, we are amateurs dreaming of the big prize. I think it's easier for a television audience to tell us apart if we're not dressed alike."

"It's so exciting. I promise, I won't make a peep. Wouldn't want to distract you, but the judges better not say anything bad about your baking or they'll have me to deal with."

"Gran, the judges give critiques when they taste each product. They can be quite critical."

"Humph, I'm just saying."

Tyler turned into the driveway, scanned the parking lot, swung around to the front entrance. "Wow, lots of cars. A semi behind the building—looks like they're carting in folding chairs. And, look at the TV crew. Star, this is the big time. Mrs. Bloom—"

"Tyler, please call me Mary, although I quite like Madame."

"Very well, Madame Mary, save me a seat, if you please. Star, text me when you know what time the last bakeoff begins—your taffy pull? My parents would like to come, cheer you on. If that's okay with you?"

"Invite them to join us as early as they like. And, Ty … thanks for the good luck hanky."

Chapter 43

COMMOTION FILLED the baking hall.

Movers aligned fifty or so folding chairs in two rows, staggered so everyone could see the action.

The cameramen, who had been filming from the start, were positioned on the sleds making last minute adjustments.

Three cable network crews jockeyed for position on either side of the stage enabling them to swing around to the judges, the host, the bakers. With cameras hoisted on their shoulders, they could easily walk around zooming in and out for the best shot. A cameraman was ready to walk alongside a reporter interviewing the bakers, asking for a snippet of why they entered the competition, their background, and what they would do with the money if they won.

Star's heart shifted into overdrive as she settled Gran in the front row center, and then strode to her workstation swapping comments with a fiftyish woman competitor behind her. The four workstations were lined up two on either side of the aisle.

Jim and Stephanie entered from the hallway at the back of the stage followed by the two judges.

All were smiling. The cameras rolling.

"Welcome, Bakers." Jim paused looking over the scene in front of him. Each baker stood in the center of their workspace facing him. "As you can see, we have made some changes since you were last here—fewer stations, chairs for spectators, and more cameras. We are also honored to have some guests ... I suspect more of your family and friends will join us later today. A few came early." Jim nodded to Gran and two others.

"Network and cable stations are present—nothing like a little publicity I always say." Jim looked to his right, to his left, nodding to ABC's Orlando affiliate, CBS's Orlando affiliate, and Brighthouse, a cable provider for central Florida. "We also have a reporter from our local newspaper, The News Journal, Daytona Beach."

Jim nodded to the reporter.

"Thank you all. I'm sure you will enjoy the drama that is about to unfold, drama with sweet morsels, a nice benefit when you attend a baking contest. You are all invited after the contest to join in a celebration—soft drinks, and to taste the final round of baked goods.

"We had another withdrawal this morning. The contestant who burned her hand yesterday decided she could not compete on the level she felt was required to win.

"Today, the final day, you will be challenged with the task of completing entries for two episodes. The category for the first episode will be pastries, a French pastry. The second will be your choice, but something sweet, enough for fifty people to sample. If we have more than fifty guests, we will cut the products into smaller pieces so everyone has a taste. You will have two and a half hours for each category, a forty-five minute break between.

"After the grand prize is awarded, refreshments will be served, and reporters will be given a chance to interview the winner. To make it to the finals—Stephanie and I believe you are all winners.

"Declared a winner or not, with the media attention, the display of your baking talent, we believe that doors will open to you for a future in baking if you choose that path.

"So, without further adieu ... bakers, *pastry* is the category.

"Let the baking begin."

Chapter 44

STAR THREW A SMILE Gran's way then opened her little metal recipe binder. They had discussed her final entry late into the night and had decided if the category was pastry, Star would prepare Buche-de Noel, the Christmas log. A pastry the two of them baked on numerous Christmas holidays as far back as Star could remember, the pastry serving as the table's centerpiece.

After Christmas dinner, after the dishes were cleared away, Gran would cut the log, gently sliding each piece onto a china plate. Star, one by one, set a plate in front of each family member. She would then take her place next to Gran, and Gran would take the first bite to see if it was worthy of eating. Of course, it always was.

Star loved the tradition.

She set to work, first baking a thin sponge cake, rolled the cake into a cylinder, icing it to resemble a Yule log. Next she prepared the Marzipan, rolling the dough into sheets, and then separating the sheets into smaller batches to add coloring: green holly leaves, red holly berries, and dough colored mushrooms with a smudge of cocoa powder. Placing the little decorations, leaves and berries on the log, and mushrooms spaced here and there against the log, Star glanced at Gran, sharing a smile and many memories.

Star finished with a few minutes to spare.

The judges stopped at the end of each baker's counter discussing the presentation, the taste, the quality, then moved to the front of the hall.

There was no contest. Star came in first in the pastry category.

Jim declared a forty-five minute break as additional guests entered the hall, Tyler scooting in behind them. Stepping quickly, he brought a take-out sandwich and a large coffee to Star and a sandwich and smaller coffee to Gran. Star didn't think she could eat, but at Gran's urging tried a bit of ham and cheese devouring it with several bites. She was hungry after all.

Manny, Liz, and Jane sauntered in and Tyler manned-up introducing everyone to Mary, Star's grandmother. Behind several other guests and family members of the bakers, Star spotted Benny and the Butterworth sisters. Batting her eyes to keep the tears at bay, she quickly went to greet them, grasping the handles of Benny's wheelchair, guiding him to the outside edge of her workstation. "You're going to be my guardian angel, Benny," she whispered in his ear.

Benny chuckled. "I didn't know a man could be an angel."

"You're an exception, my friend. Thank you so much for coming," she said giving him a hug and a kiss on his rosy cheek.

Gran hustled up to her granddaughter. "And who is this handsome gentleman," she asked.

"Gran, meet Benny. Benny and I met the first time I went into the diner. You might say we came in together. Benny, this is my Gran."

Gran shook Benny's hand then turned to Star. "How about we *saw* up that log, give your friends a chance to sample your baking?"

"Good idea. There are paper plates, napkins, and I think I have some plastic forks ..."

Gran took her traditional place in front of the log, placed a small piece on each plate, and Star delivered pieces to her well-wishers and others until the log was gone.

The additional people filling the hall, laughing, chattering, sampling the baker's products provided a delightful scene captured by all the cameras. Reporters interviewed family members, jotting down background stories on each of the contestants.

The forty-five minute break was extended to an hour and fifteen minutes.

Chapter 45

"JIM, FOR HEAVEN'S SAKE, get over here." Stephanie stood in the back hallway grabbing his arm as he strolled by with an empty plate, licking his lips as he popped the last piece of a Marzipan mushroom in his mouth. She pulled him into an empty room that in its history had been a storeroom.

"What's wrong? Did you try—"

"We're dead!"

"What do you mean we're dead?"

"Oh, I don't know ... like in broke, no contract, not one network wants us, kinda like we're skewered ... hung out to dry."

"Okay with the metaphors. I'll ask you again and please, specifics this time. What happened?"

"Our agent called. Our last chance for a contract came in negative. He tried them all again, anyone who had shown interest. The networks, the cable outlets, free lancers—all said no. What are we going to do?" Stephanie paced the dusty room, looked out a grimy window, hands planted on her hips.

Jim, fingers laced behind his neck, blew out a long blast of air. How had it come to this? He knew he had a good reality series. The series was perfect for television, but his timing was bad. Down economy. Networks were not about to take a chance on something new. Hell, they weren't going to gamble on some new producer out of the blue. They were staying with what they knew, something tried and true, a producer with a track record of creating winners.

"So, Jim ... hello ... Stephanie to Jim. I asked you, what are we going to do?"

"First, we say nothing until the winner is named. We tell the winner we'll talk after everyone is gone—the judges, the camera guys, the rental van. The reporters don't have to know. They have their story. The rental company will pick up everything as per the agreement. All the equipment will be loaded into the semi parked out back. They've been given instructions to pack up everything else dropping it off at a church in Port Orange—a donation. What the church can't use they're free to hold a fundraiser. Whatever. I just want it gone. The crew will get their checks in the mail. If they balk, we tell them that in the excitement we didn't get their checks cut."

"Yeah? And the winner?"

"We tell the winner the truth, God knows we tried. There is no money. We'll write up a note that we owe the money. That's show business, Steph. Sometimes the show closes before it opens. Come on, let's finish the production. Remember, we still have a great show...maybe someday..." Jim threw his hands in the air, marched down the hall, marched into the makeshift studio.

All eyes were trained on the host—the bakers, the guests, the cameras, the reporters.

Chapter 46

JIM MARCHED TO the center of the stage, snatched up the microphone, and addressed the audience.

"Well, here we are. The final bakeoff. The final episode. What a journey it's been."

He looked around. *Great crowd.*

"Okay, What do you say? Shall we get on with it?"

A chorus yelled out, "YES!"

Jim smiled, took a deep breath. "Remember, you are all invited to stay for refreshments, congratulate the winner, and wish all the competitors good luck.

"Bakers, are you ready?"

Again the chorus, "YES!"

"Something sweet ... your choice.

"Bakers, let the baking begin."

Wanda and Charlie, along with Tyler's parents, quietly entered the hall, saw Tyler, waved at him, and joined Star's cheering section.

With images of Tyler in his mom's kitchen, Star smiled at him, at his mom and dad. They nodded in return sharing her thoughts. Ty was dying to tell her his news, but not now. This was Star's big moment.

Gran's taffy was her ace in the hole.

If she didn't come in number one with this, then she would have given it her all, and she could walk away knowing she had done her best.

Benny didn't say a word, his eyes following every move Star made. Nodding encouragement if she looked his way, his face lighting up when she pulled and pulled the taffy to reach the consistency where she could separate the large band into separate portions. He was still grinning when she added the flavorings turning the taffy lemon yellow, lime green, but the red and white strip was pure magic.

Time was running out.

Star scurried from side to side, lining up the scissors, wax paper, apothecary jars for the final push. Working with one section at a time, pulling it out to about one and a half inches wide, three-quarters of an inch thick, she cut the section into pieces with the scissors, wrapped each piece in wax paper, twisted the ends of the paper to seal, and dropped it into the jar. On to the next piece. The final section was the striped peppermint.

Almost finished.

Jim called out, "Time's up! Put your entry to the end of the counter for the judges and return to the center of your station."

Star put the lid on the last jar, lining it up with the others at the end of the counter.

She made it with two seconds to spare.

Wiping her hands on her frilly apron, she turned to Benny handing him a piece of the striped peppermint that he loved. His gnarled fingers reached for her hand, kissed her fingers. "Thank you, Star. You were wonderful. Just look at those jars. I swear they're twinkling at the judges."

The judges seemed to take forever, stopping to chat with each competitor, wishing them good luck, and telling them how much they had enjoyed tasting their products. After making the rounds, the judges held a conference in the back room with the producers, finally emerging with their results.

Jim picked up the microphone, looked around at the array of cameras, the guests. Then he turned to the bakers.

"The judges said it was a difficult decision and they appreciated your efforts, and believe you have the talent to pursue a successful career in baking. But, they also felt one of you stood out from the rest, deserving to be the winner of the Florida Amateur Baking Competition ... and that baker is ... Star Bloom."

Tyler was the first to reach her, picking her up in a fierce hug, twirling her around. "Congratulations, my little baker girl. Of course, I knew all along you'd pull off a win." He set her on her feet, gave her a smooch smack on her lips surprising them both. Star, face flushed from her victory, or was it his kiss, beamed at her friend as reporters broke into their personal celebration.

"Wait, wait, Benny. Benny, are you okay? Be careful everybody, this man is my special friend. Don't trample him."

"I've got him, Star," Tyler said, grabbing the handles of the wheelchair. "We're going to help ourselves to the refreshments. Right, Benny?"

"Right, Tyler ... over there with the Butterworth sisters."

The melee continued around Star.

Television crews followed their reporters, taking pictures of Star Bloom then of the other finalists. The News Journal Reporter asked a few questions, told her he'd do a follow-up story in a few days.

No one noticed the movers hauling everything, piece by piece, out of the hall. No one noticed the semi-truck rolling out of the parking lot, or the large van loaded with camera gear following the truck.

Finally the chatter died down as the party began to break up. The reporters, cable and network news, along with the reporter from the News Journal, left to submit their stories. Charlie and Wanda left, driving Benny and the Butterworth sisters back to the diner. Liz, Manny, and Jane beamed at Star, shaking their heads, blown away by what their friend had accomplished, and with one last hug left the hall, an apothecary jar of lemon taffy under Jane's arm.

Tyler's parents hugged Star, and hoped she'd be over for pizza again soon. They wanted to know all the gory behind-the-scene details. Cindy cradled the jar of lime taffy as she and Tony said goodbye.

Gran hugged her granddaughter, whispering in her ear, that they would begin plans to lease the little bakery.

Tyler said he'd wait by the door for her. He thought maybe a little more celebrating would be nice.

Star turned as Jim and Stephanie approached. "Quite a day, Star," Jim said. "Congratulations." He looked around for a place to sit, but the hall was bare. "Those men certainly cleared everything out in record time. We don't even have a chair to sit on. Stephanie and I want to talk to you, to tell you—"

Stephanie jumped in. Jim was such a wimp. "Star the good news is you won the competition. The bad news is that the contract we thought we had to syndicate the show fell through. There is no money. We put up most of the cash to produce the competition. If it's any consolation to you, we lost all that money. We're broke."

Stephanie paused, took a deep breath, and pulled a folded envelope from her shoulder bag. "Jim and I wrote up a promissory note, good for a year, after that ... well, maybe sometime in the future. We won't forget you. You'll be the first we contact if any interest in the show crops up."

Stephanie gave the envelope to Star, then stuck her hand out as did Jim.

Star shook their hands, a mechanical reaction.

"Wait. You can't be serious. Is this some kind of sick joke?"

"It's not a joke. We're sorry. Jim's phone number is at the bottom of the note. If you have any questions call him. Come on, Jim, let's get out of here."

Jim dutifully followed in Stephanie's wake, turning with one last thought. "That Christmas log, what did you call it, Buche de Noel, was out of this world. Can you send me the recipe?"

Star, standing with the promissory note in hand, stared at the producers as they shot out of the hall.

Tyler stood at the front door waiting to drive the winner home, maybe stop for a celebratory dinner, definitely tell her his news. He was excited, but at the same time filled with sadness. He was leaving Star.

Standing where the stage had been, standing in the empty hall, Star blinked. Was it all a dream?

When Stephanie and Jim brushed by Tyler at the door, he looked around for Star. He took a step into the empty hall and stopped. Something was wrong. She wasn't smiling, almost like she was hypnotized. Fearing she was going to keel over, he slowly approached her.

"Hey, Star, it's me. Your Gran is waiting in the car. Are you sick ... what's wrong?"

Seeing her dream of the little bakery fading away, she looked up.

"What's wrong? Everything!

"There's *no* prize money."

Tyler took hold of her shoulders. "Look at me, Miss Bloom." He gently lifted her chin his deep brown eyes looking into her blue eyes filled with disbelief, searching his face for answers.

"You won today. There are going to be many news outlets reporting your win by morning. Those stories will spawn more stories. Now, come on. Your Gran is waiting in the car."

Star nodded.

Tyler walked her out of the cement-block building. Gran was leaning against the car, her wide smile disappearing as she caught sight of the pair walking toward her. It was not a triumphant march. She opened her arms as Star reached her. "Sweetie, what's wrong?" Gran looked over her granddaughter's shoulder to Ty. He was shaking his head as he opened the back door of the car.

Star pulled back. "Gran, the contract to syndicate the show fell through. Jim said there's no money. In fact, he and Stephanie are broke."

"That's awful. How long have they been perpetrating this fraud?"

Tyler had to smile at the crusty side of Madame Bloom.

"I don't know when they found out, but from the way they acted I would say they were in shock, so maybe last night ... even today. How can I win and lose at the same time, Gran?"

"Now you listen to me, sweetie." Gran slid into the backseat making room for Star to follow.

Tyler climbed in behind the wheel and turned to be a partner in the conversation.

Gran picked up Star's hand. "With all the publicity, those news people who were there today filming the two episodes, the story of your winning, decisively I might add, something is bound to happen."

Star pulled the letter from her tote handing it to her grandmother who quickly read the few handwritten lines.

"Tyler, did you read this?" Gran asked handing him the piece of paper. "You see, Star, it still might happen. They gave you a promissory note ... they intend to make good on your winning."

"Only if they sell the show, Gran. Stephanie sure didn't sound or act like that was going to happen."

Gran patted Star's hand as Tyler handed the letter back. "Just so you know, Star my dear precious granddaughter, I'm not leaving just yet. Let's see what happens when the news of your winning hits the news wires. What do you think, Tyler?"

"My thoughts exactly. Star is a winner and tomorrow morning everyone will know it."

Starting the Lincoln, he pulled out of the empty driveway, turning north on Williamson Boulevard, then east on International Speedway to the ocean. His news would have to wait another day.

Chapter 47

WORD SPREAD RAPIDLY.

The producers of the much-hyped pilot of the reality television series featuring amateur bakers had fled town and, worse, they had reneged on the top prize: $50,000. The old phrase, *that's show business*, was bandied about with a shrug.

The lesson—if it sounds too good to be true then it probably is. That's life.

The fact that the winner of the competition, Star Bloom, was one of their own, gave grist to the television, radio, and print reporters. The winner turned loser was the morning's lead story.

Tyler drove up to the curb, throttled the Harley's engine twice, waiting for her to step out the door. Star put on a brave smile as she hopped on the seat behind him, arms around his waist, head resting on his back. He would have loved her resting against him if it wasn't because she was so sad.

Entering the diner, Charlie first, then Wanda with tears in her eyes, told her how sorry they were. They couldn't believe that nice man who chatted with them over refreshments could be such a scoundrel.

Star felt worse as the day wore on. Everybody felt terrible hearing the news, hugged her, told her not to worry. She was a winner for God's sake.

Tyler watched her receiving the hugs, the condolences, always responding with a smile, thanking everyone for their concern.

Benny, the Butterworth sisters, couldn't believe how the producers could perpetrate such a fraud—the same words Gran had used.

She closed her eyes, fought back the urge to cry when Jane, Liz, and Manny arrived for lunch, ostensibly for lunch, but really to offer their support. In every instance, she said the producers meant well, they simply had lost their investors and were never given a contract to sign.

The turnover of the seating at the diner was constant. *Thank heaven for that,* Star thought wondering if she might run out of meatball mini-tarts. She did run out of cranberries, substituting an orange marmalade glaze. Putting the plate up on the order window for Tyler, she noted there were no more tickets hanging on the wire, no orders waiting to be filled. She chuckled—every ticket had included a smiley face at the bottom. Tyler's way of trying to cheer her up.

Wanda asked Star to sit down for a cup of coffee.

Wiping her hands on her apron, sliding into the booth opposite Wanda, she thanked Ty for the coffee.

Wanda looked up at Tyler over the rim of her coffee mug. "Please join us. I have something to tell you and Star."

Ty slid in next to Star. "That was some rush we had this morning. Those kids loved your mini-tarts. Everyone did. And all your ..." Tyler stopped talking. Were those tears in Wanda's eyes?

Wanda looked wistfully at Tyler. What a treasure—not really a boy, almost thirty. But he seemed like a boy with his cartoons, his clever way of turning a phrase. "I'll tell you straight up, no point in beating around the bush. Charlie and I are closing the diner after Labor Day. It will be the end of summer and the rush of tourists will be gone. We're putting the diner up for sale."

Wanda looked down, reached for the little plastic box next to the wall—tapped the sugar packets noting they had to be replenished as she pulled out a white paper napkin.

Star reached for Wanda's hand. "Business is good, why—"

"We're burned out. Charlie isn't well. Too much, it's just too much work for us ... to keep it going. Charlie wanted to tell you himself, but he couldn't face you. He says you two are like his children, children we never had."

Ty looked at Star. Another blow to her. And he still hadn't told her he was leaving. Yesterday wasn't the right time, and now this. Tomorrow? "I'm sorry, Wanda. But now that your business is booming, and with your location … I mean right across the street from all the action—Bandshell, Ferris wheel, the beach—you should be able to clear enough to, to, maybe retire." His brows raised, eyes hopeful. "Don't you think?"

"Maybe. Thank you, Tyler. Oh, and the robber is in custody. The police picked him last night at the bus station. He had a ticket to Miami in his pocket."

"That's a relief," Tyler said.

"Yes, your drawing was a big help. Detective Watson called Charlie this morning, wanted him to come identify the guy in a lineup."

"And did he?" Star asked.

"Yes, without a doubt. Oops, here's that family and their little ones. Better give them your special drawing placemats, Ty."

The shift ended. The new part-time cook Wanda hired while Star was competing drifted in to relieve her. She briefed him on what to expect from the dinner crowd. Rain was predicted which meant the diner would be rocking. The diner was a great place to kill time until the rain stopped.

Tyler told Star to wait inside. He had a couple of rain slickers stored in the bike. Dashing back in, he helped her on with the yellow slicker, promising to drive slowly. She'd be home in less than five minutes, beats walking and getting soaked.

Pulling to the curb in front of her building, he turned off the key, hopped off to help her. Removing the slicker, she thanked him for the ride, turned to dash inside.

He grasped her arm. "Star—dinner tomorrow? My studio. I have something to show you."

"Okay, tomorrow. Bye."

Chapter 48

STAR OPENED HER front door to the homey aroma of Gran's fresh baked meatloaf, glazed with sesame-ginger sauce, and a side of garlicky mashed potatoes.

"Gran, you'll never know how much I love you," she said drawing her grandmother into a warm hug.

"I love you too, sweetie ... more than you'll ever know. Now, throw those greasy smelling clothes in the hamper, take a quick shower if you like while I open a bottle of wine I bought from the nice liquor store up the street. Then, I want to hear about your day."

Star gave Gran another hug. "I won't be long. Go ahead and pour."

When Star stepped out of the bathroom in her fuzzy sky-blue bathrobe, a towel wrapped around her wet hair, she saw Gran had pulled out all the stops trying to cheer her up. A candle flickered happily in the center of her second-hand bistro table.

Gran handed her a goblet of wine. "Now you sit while I serve up our dinner. I heard the news on the television after you left this morning. All the reporters were talking about you. I bet some of your friends stopped by the diner."

"Some? How about all. They were so nice ... it was awful. You'll never guess the bombshell Wanda laid on Ty and me. She and Charlie are closing the diner after Labor Day. The end of summer. Putting it up for sale."

"Oh, dear. It must be hard for them … or maybe a relief. Charlie didn't look all that well yesterday at the … you know…"

"Yeah, you can say it … at the bakeoff. You're right, though. Wanda said they were tired, couldn't handle it anymore. She said Charlie wasn't well."

"So, no little bakery, and now you have to find another job. Labor day's only two weeks away."

"Sucks doesn't it. Sorry, I didn't mean—"

"Sweetie, it does *suck*. How can I help? Pick up some newspapers tomorrow? Are there any that handle jobs in the food industry more than others?"

"Maybe I should give up."

"You don't mean move back to Hoboken?"

"No. I'm not that desperate … yet."

"Star, you just won a competition. It wasn't easy. Baking is in your blood—"

"But, Gran … no prize money. No job—signs I'm not meant to—"

"Voodoo nonsense! You have to be patient."

"How patient? I can't pay the bills with hope."

"Okay. Let's say … give it one month. One month *after* the diner closes. Maybe they'll change their minds. Now, let's not beat a dead horse. I'm changing the subject."

"Gran, what would I do without you?" Swirling the wine goblet in the candlelight, little dashes of red popped through the glass. "I'm glad you're here … maybe I can trick myself."

"Trick yourself?"

"Yeah … like I'm on an upswing."

"Star, we never had a chance to talk about Ash, the man you mentioned several times when we chatted over the phone. Last thing you said to me was that his grandmother flew over from London to help him. I couldn't believe how you described his saving your life. Thank God he was there."

Star took their plates to the sink, rinsed them, put them in the dishwasher. "He's a Muslim, Gran. A good man. A man on a mission."

"What kind of mission, dear?"

"To paraphrase his grandmother, Ash turned away from the militant ways of his family in Syria."

"Syria? Oh my goodness."

"Yup. Turned out his mother and her mother schemed to be sure he was born in the States ... the Bronx. His grandmother and grandfather paid for his education ... Master's Degree in Media Communication, so he could be the voice for Muslims here in the U.S., a voice to tell Americans the other side of the story, a story that most Muslims are peaceful and would never want to hurt our country. Anyway, he left for Miami, and then in a few months is going on to Detroit ... and ... I don't know ... travel around the country."

"My, my ... such dedication. It wouldn't have worked, you know." Gran topped off their wine.

"Tell me why not, Gran. I want you to tell me."

Gran could see that Star was conflicted, but also trying to come to grips with losing someone to a cause, someone she cared for.

"Sounds to me like two people with strong ambitions were drawn to each other, but their ambitions didn't align. Ash must have seen that but couldn't bring himself to alter his course. Powerful thing when you feel an obligation to a cause, a mission bigger than your life, a calling if you will."

"We never kissed—he touched my arm, I took his hand, pulled him along the beach. Yet, I was attracted to him and I felt he was to me."

"It hasn't been long ... his leaving. How do you feel now?"

"The first episode of the bakeoff finished the day before the robbery. Everything happened so fast after that. Fast, but I felt like I was going through a time warp in slow motion. Police, accusations, his grandmother, then he was gone. Was he real? Yes. A forever memory. You're right, I guess. It was not to be but Manny said I'm a richer person for having known him."

"And, my dearest granddaughter, Ash is richer for having known you. Now, let's get some sleep. Are you sure you're okay on that lumpy couch of yours?"

"I'm sure. Sorry about the bed, if you can call a blowup mattress a bed."

Gran chuckled. "You should have seen your grandfather's and my first apartment. It was about on a par with yours."

"Before I forget, Tyler wants to show me something. He asked me to dinner at his studio tomorrow after work. Maybe a new cartoon ... like the little baker girl losing."

"Hey sweetie, you're on an upswing, remember?"

Chapter 49

IT HAD BECOME one of his favorite things to do—transporting Star on the back of his Harley, her arms wrapped about his waist, her head leaning into his back. He could envision her hair floating out from under her helmet on the wind.

Pulling into his driveway, they both hopped off, running up the steps to his studio to escape the soupy humidity.

"What smells so good? Italian for sure."

"Mom's spaghetti and meatballs. I told her we'd pick something up on the way, but, when she heard you were coming over to have dinner with me, she insisted. Spaghetti is in the slow cooker on the counter, and ... yup ... Italian bread with garlic butter is in the micro ready to be zapped."

"Looks like she opened a bottle of Merlot ... letting it breeeathe."

"That would be Dad. Are you hungry?"

"After cooking all day I can't believe it, but, yes I'm hungry. How about a glass of wine first. You said you had some news. Tell me, Superman. Give."

A rash of nerves ran through Tyler's stomach. All of sudden he didn't want to tell her because then it would be real. He'd be leaving. He kept telling himself it wasn't forever, but it felt like forever.

Star perched on the high stool at the counter holding a wine glass out to him. Tyler poured, pulled up another stool at the end of the counter so he faced her. His Kewpie doll was now a woman, a woman he loved. He had to be careful, not say *those* words. Not now, maybe never, but definitely not tonight.

He didn't know how she was going to take his news. She'd be happy for him, for sure. Because he was her friend. Now that Ash was gone, he didn't know if she had another friend, or friends. She never said, and he pretty much knew what she did every day, every hour.

"I told you I was applying to some small animated film companies. There are a few that receive subcontracts from Disney, Pixar, and DreamWorks—the biggies."

"Ty, someone wants to interview you? I'm not surprised. You are sooo talented. They'd be lucky—"

"I had an offer. I accepted it ... I ... I'm leaving for Burbank in a week."

"Burbank? As in Burbank, California?"

"Yes. I signed a one-year contract with a small animation company, to be a member of their team working on a new DreamWorks project. They liked how I bring animated characters to life—their feelings, their emotions. Star, they actually told me that."

"Ty, that's incredible. Your dream. How long have you known ... why didn't you tell me ..."

"You had a lot going on, the bakeoff ... and stuff. You'll never guess what caught their eye, what they really liked? Why I was selected."

"What?"

"My story—The Little Baker Girl."

Star gave him a soft punch on the shoulder. "You've never mentioned that title before. You have to show it to me."

"Okay, but after we have something to eat."

"No, Mr. Tyler Jackman, A-K-A Superman. Now!" Sliding off her perch, she gave him a warm hug. Remembering the kiss, she quickly backed away, giggling, her face flushed. "Now, Ty. Show me the clip."

Tyler's heart was racing. God, she almost kissed him.

"Okay, okay. It's your story ... the little baker girl ... her name is Star. The California group loved it. But it's not finished, she's a series of frames." Turning on his computer, the first frame appeared on the big television screen mounted on the wall above his computer. "I drew you as a Kewpie doll."

"Oh, I love that doll. I had one when I was little ... Gran gave her to me."

"So, I created you cooking your first egg over easy—"

"The one that hit the wall?"

"Yup, then all the stuff with the meatball mini-tarts."

"Oh, there's Jane. Perfect ... her pink hair glowing."

"I took some artistic license with the robbery ... a serpent grabbing you, and then ... well, a tabby with glasses, that would be me, saved you. Then I added your description of the first episode of the bakeoff, sitting on the floor watching your pie in the oven. There are some other clips I haven't finished, but that's the gist of it."

Shutting down his computer, he turned to her.

"So, what do you think? OK?"

"Way better than OK. I love it."

"Whew. Time for some of Mom's spa ... hey, what's the matter?" Picking up a dishtowel, he dabbed at a tear meandering down her cheek.

"I'm just happy for you. Honest."

"You don't look happy?"

"You leave in a week?"

"That's the plan."

"You're not going to stop working at the diner are you, I mean tomorrow or any of the days before you put on your cape, and, and go to save some other damsel in distress?"

"I'll pick you up every day, bring you home after every shift."

"Promise?"

"Tyler Jackman's word is his bond ... now, my little Kewpie doll, let's eat."

He turned to the slow cooker. He couldn't look at her. What was he doing? He loved her. He had accepted a job—hours, miles, the whole country away. He jabbed at the buttons on the microwave to warm the bread.

She hadn't moved.

"Come on, Superman," he muttered under his breath. "This is the job you've dreamed of. You are going."

Chapter 50

"THANKS, TY, FOR DINNER." Star hopped off the Harley, saying goodnight over her shoulder, not daring to look at him.

Gran was at the door. She waved to Tyler as Star raced by her. Were those tears she saw? Closing the door she heard her granddaughter sobbing. She was lying on the bed sobbing. Star never cried.

Gran knelt on the floor by the mattress, reached out, gently patting Star's back, trying to comfort her.

"Star, honey, what's the matter?"

"Everything is the matter, Gran. My world is crumbling in front of my eyes and I can't stop it." Star rolled over, sat up against the wall.

Gran held out a tissue, crawled up on the mattress, leaned against the wall beside her. Star laid her head on her grandmother's shoulder, swiping at her tears.

"You texted me when you and Tyler left the diner. Nothing seemed wrong. What happened?"

"Gran, I'm so mixed up. I don't know who I am, I don't know what I want, but it doesn't seem to matter because it's all falling apart around me."

"But, dear, why all of a sudden—"

"Ty's leaving. He accepted a job in California. Gran it hurts. He's done everything for me, everything with me—my God, Gran, what am I going to do?"

Star slumped over, laying her head on her grandmother's lap, tears flowing again. "What's wrong with me? I thought I was falling in love with Ash. He left me—it hurt—but not like this. Why didn't I see it—Ty made me laugh, he talked to me, he was open about his dreams, we dreamed together. He's been there for me all summer. He was with me when I found out there was no prize money. Gran, I think I'm in love with him."

"Did you tell him you love him?" Gran asked, stroking her hair.

Star sat up, mopping her face with the daisy-flowered blanket. Misery covering her face, her tear-filled eyes looking at her grandmother. "I can't, Gran. I think he cares about me so I can't say anything that would put a cloud over his taking a new job, dampen his excitement. He's wanted to work in the film industry, in animation, since he was a little boy. I have to show him I'm happy for him. Supportive." Fresh tears erupted.

"Yes, well, I don't know ..."

"He signed a one-year contract. Gran, he's leaving in a week."

"I see. A year isn't forever. I can understand you're not wanting to tell him you love him ... not just yet, anyway. And, well ... you said yourself you were shocked how hard the news he was leaving hit you." Gran sighed.

"I think a little time, time to sort out your feelings, get your feet firmly on the ground—they certainly have been knocked out from under you the past few weeks. But it's not as if he's falling off the earth, you know. You can talk on the phone, and there's the texting thing you two do all the time. Yes, a little space would be good. I do think you can be honest with him. Tell him you care he's going away. You want to keep in touch. Even suggest when you might see each other again. Christmas would be nice. What do you think?"

"The holidays? Surely he would come home for the holidays."

"Look at his new job as a blessing. Give you both time to think. And, you have a lot to do here."

"Yeah, like finding a job."

Star hugged her grandmother. Kissed her cheek. "Thank you. I think I can make it to the holidays."

"I know you can, dear."

Chapter 51

IT WAS A ROUTINE DAY—a quick hug and a peck on Gran's cheek, reminding her she would be a little late tonight—she and Ty were going to take a walk on the beach after closing. Star hurried out the door, Gran calling after her that she'd be down to the diner to share a cup of coffee with Benny.

All routine.

Star threw her leg over the back seat rest of Ty's Harley, wrapped her arms around him, and laid her head against his back. Ty eased on the gas bringing the Harley to a noisy pitch, swinging away from the curb, roaring up the street.

All routine.

Not!

Star felt Ty's heart pounding through his ribs.

He felt her heart pounding against his back.

It was the last day they would see each other. He was flying out of Orlando early in the morning, flying to start a new adventure, a new life, fulfilling a dream he'd carried since he was a little boy. A little boy lying on the floor, a box of crayons scattered around him. His chubby fist gripped one color after the other, making marks on a pad of paper almost as big as he was.

On the one hand he was terrified that he might not succeed, on the other exhilarated about the opportunity of joining the group in Burbank. All that, and at the same time a sense of sadness. Why does life have to be so hard? Why does the thrill of achieving your dream have to be accompanied by the angst of loss?

Throughout the day Charlie's diner rocked. The Wurly belted out song after song, the neon lights jumping in rhythm. Hungry tourists mixed with regulars, standing in a line that snaked out to the sidewalk—the last weekend of summer packed with fun on the beach.

Gran, beating the breakfast crowd, sat with Benny. She ordered a stack of pancakes. Her stomach was a bit jumpy knowing what her granddaughter was going through today—her best friend leaving. She cleaned her plate, finished her coffee.

"Same time tomorrow, Benny?"

"I'll have your coffee waiting, Mary," he said with a wink.

Gran hugged Tyler and wished him great success. As she left, the Butterworth sisters bustled in. Whispering back and forth, they decided to sit at the table with Benny. A family had taken up residence in their favorite booth and they didn't want to wait. They ordered their usual diet breakfast—pancakes, meatball mini-tarts with spicy cranberry sauce, and an egg over easy.

The younger sister, Hattie, looked up at Tyler as he set their plates, lined up on his arm, on the table. "Tyler, we heard you're leaving, and my sister and I wondered if we could buy the cartoon on the wall—our cartoon. We just think it looks so cute, and you captured us perfectly."

"I don't know. Let me ask Star. She's the one who had the cartoons framed. I'm sure it will be okay."

"Of course, Tyler, you have to autograph it for us. Will it be hard to pop it out of the frame?"

"No. I can do it in a jiffy. Enjoy your breakfast ... I'll ask Star."

Star was flipping an order of pancakes, when Tyler whispered in her ear. She smiled at the sisters.

The sisters left with their treasure, giggling as they strolled out of the diner into a beautiful sunny day.

Then Benny wanted his cartoon. Tyler had to sign it, of course.

Then word began to circulate, that the waiter was the artist of the cartoons on the wall ... and the cartoons on the back of the paper placemats ... and that he was off to Burbank, California ... and that he must be going to work for Pixar, DreamWorks, no, silly ... for Disney.

The line had dwindled by ten thirty when Jane, with Manny and Liz in tow, arrived.

Jane saw Tyler signing the front of Benny's cartoon. She strutted over to Benny, her pink lips bowed sweetly, when she asked Tyler for her cartoon on the wall.

The remaining guests then wanted in on the action. Before lunch the walls were bare, every framed cartoon had been carried out the door—quarters fed to the Wurlitzer on the way in, a signed cartoon under their arms going out.

The placemats were next. Before the late lunch crowd left, exhausted from several hours on the beach, they were not too tired to snatch up a few, with the artist's autograph as a souvenir of their summer vacation.

Wanda asked Tyler to tally up the register. Most of the guests had paid in cash. Charlie wanted to deposit the bills in the bank, fearing a repeat of the robbery a few weeks ago.

Tyler went through the routine of cashing out the register.

"Hey, Star, There's an envelope addressed to you," he called over his shoulder, stuffing the bills in the deposit bag along with tally sheet.

"Where?"

"Leaning between the register and my order pads. Here." He handed the deposit bag to Wanda, and then waved the white business envelope at Star through the order window.

"Thanks." Star set the envelope aside against the pepper shaker, flipped three burgers, reached for the buns, laying them on the grill to warm up. Plating the order, the last for the moment, she reached for the envelope. Wiping pieces of onion off a paring knife, she slit the envelope open.

Tyler came around the corner just as Star sank to the floor, leaning against the stainless steel cabinet under the grill. Her fingers were shaking, her blue eyes big as saucers. Tyler dropped to the floor beside her, the heat of the grill warming his already sweaty back.

"What is it? Bad news?"

She raised her hand to his, the piece of paper shaking so badly Ty had to steady her fingers releasing the paper in his hand.

"My God, Star! This is a check for a ... a ... a hundred thousand dollars."

Star couldn't move, only her eyes moved, looking at him. "Do you think it's real?"

"Yeah. It's a cashier's check made out to you, Star Bloom."

"There's no signature. Who—"

"It's drawn on the Bank of America. Star, I'm sure it's real. Come on. We'll ask Charlie and Wanda to take over for us ... a short break. There's a branch on the next block."

Tyler jumped up, extending his hand to Star as she handed him the envelope. Tyler told Wanda they had to go on a quick errand, all the orders were filled.

Star's heart was pounding. She was sure it would punch through her chest if she didn't faint first.

There were two people ahead of them at the bank teller's window. Tyler asked a woman sitting at a computer outside the bank manager's office, if she had bottled water. His friend felt a little sick. The woman nodded, walked down a hall, returning with an icy bottle.

Tyler hurried back to Star, twisted off the cap. "Here, take a few sips."

"Ty, it ... the check is dated two days ago. It has to be a joke, a very sick joke."

"You'll know in a minute. We're next."

"May I help you?"

Star laid the envelope on the counter. Her fingers shaking so badly, that Ty reached for the envelope, removed the check, handing it to the teller.

Star leaned against the counter, locked her eyes on the teller. "Is it real?" she asked, her voice barely audible.

The lady picked it up, scrutinized it, her head tilting. "Yes, it's real. Are you Star Bloom?"

Star nodded.

Tyler put his arm around her as she sank against him.

"Do you have an account with us, Miss Bloom? Proof of identification? Driver's license?"

Star nodded she did. Pulling her body up straight, sliding off her shoulder bag, she retrieved her checkbook, and handed it to the teller along with her Florida Driver's license.

"I'd like to deposit the ... the check into my account, please," she told the teller.

"Do you want to break—"

"All of it ... please. And, can you tell me who gave me this check?"

"Sure. It didn't originate at this branch so let me make a phone call. While I'm calling, here's a deposit slip. You'll have to endorse the back of the check—write for Deposit Only, and then your name."

Star picked up the pen the teller gave her, returned her license to her purse, looked up at Tyler, shook her head at how unbelievable this was, and signed the back of the check.

The teller returned, checked the signature and the deposit ticket. She scanned it through a computer returning the credit slip to Star, proof that $100,032 was her new balance. "I'm sorry, Miss Bloom. But the bank has strict instructions that the person who originated this cashier's check was to remain anonymous."

"Thank you for checking."

Star and Tyler strolled out of the bank, sat on a bench outside of the 7-Eleven next door. She called Gran. Repeating the story three times.

"Well, this changes everything, dear. My, my, let me sit, get my bearings. Where are you now?"

"Ty and I are sitting outside the 7-Eleven. He just went in to get me a bottle of milk."

"Milk?"

"Yeah, he said I need something to settle my nerves. No more caffeine today."

"Well ... I'm going to stay to help you, dear. We'll go lease that bakery ... if I'm going to stay to help you get your bakery up and running ... well, we have to get an apartment with walls ... and I think we have to buy a car. One car should do it, don't you think? A little sporty model. Red."

Star was laughing so hard, her sides ached. "Oh, Gran, you're priceless. I love you so much, and yes, yes, yes, to all your ideas—make that a used sporty red car. Oh, one more thing. Ty and I are going back to the diner to finish up the day. He wants to tell Wanda and Charlie goodbye and thank them for supporting him—cartoons on the walls, and placemats for the kids."

"That's nice. I'll wait up for you. And, Star, I'm so proud of you. I love you ... and ... aren't we going to have fun?"

"Yes, Gran, we're going to have a blast."

Chapter 52

TY HAD DONE so much for her. He'd been there when she needed someone, not just anyone, someone to dry her tears, someone to make her laugh. He was the one who helped with her dream. She couldn't imagine a day without Tyler Jackman. The thought of Ty going away, their time together ending ... an empty feeling washed over her.

Leaving the 7-Eleven, they strolled back to the diner sipping a small bottle of chocolate milk. Star told Tyler she didn't want to say anything to Wanda and Charlie about the money.

The final two hours slowed to a trickle at the diner. Cleaning the grill, Star glanced out the order window at Tyler. He was perched on a counter stool ready to jump if a straggler came in. He had a pen in his hand, poised over a placemat, slow at first then picking up speed, the pen flying back and forth over the paper.

Charlie suggested to Wanda they close for the night. It was eight o'clock, a concert was scheduled at the Bandshell, and he was tired.

Tyler folded the placemat, stuffing it into his pants pocket as Charlie shuffled up to him, shook his hand then pulled Ty into a hug. Wanda had tears in her eyes as she said goodbye making him promise to keep in touch.

Crossing Atlantic Avenue, Star and Tyler strolled hand in hand down the path to the beach. It was a beautiful warm night, although a bit humid. No storm clouds, only a large moon and bright stars.

The concert had started—beating drums, fingers strumming guitars accompanied an energetic vocal group. The music boomed from large speakers over the crowd, over the sandy beach, down to the gentle lapping of the waves riding the outgoing tide.

It was a magical night.

Finding a spot where the sand curved up, they sat nestling into the dip, the sand still warm from the afternoon sun.

"Who do you suppose gave you the money?" Ty asked, his hands folded across his stomach as he gazed up at the star-filled sky.

"I don't know anybody who would have that kind of money," Star said. Mimicking Ty, her hands folded, looking up, "Except maybe Jane. But with a grandniece or nephew on the way ... besides, she already did so much for me. Who do you think?"

"Well, I thought about my parents. But Dad is investing a lot in a design of a new micro-chip, and the real estate market has really turned down. Mom's appointment book is practically empty. I doubt they'd be investing in anything right now."

"You really can't call it an investment. Anonymous isn't exactly an investor of record. I saw you sketching before we left the diner. A character for your new job?"

Ty reached in his pocket, pulled out the folded placemat, handed it to her. He didn't look at her just kept staring at the moon.

Star unfolded the paper, pressed out the folds. Lips turning up, her finger traced his pen strokes of a Kewpie doll standing in front of a bakery display case. The glass shelves held plates of cookies—bourbon balls, chocolate-coconut rounds. The cookies she baked in the finals of the competition. Sitting on top of the case were three apothecary jars filled with taffy pieces wrapped in wax paper, ends twisted. The little baker girl was smiling, a puffy white baker hat on her head, slipping to the side. She was holding out a striped piece of peppermint taffy.

Reaching for Ty's hand as she looked at the cartoon, Star whispered, "It's perfect. After Gran and I get the little bakery set up, I'm framing this. It will be the first thing I hang on the wall."

"Oh. I'll draw another one. This has folds, and I dribbled a spot of coffee, and now there's sand and—"

"Ty, I said it's perfect. Perfect—folds, spot, and sand. Our night."

Ty stood, grasped her hand, pulling her up, slowly wrapping her in his arms. His embrace was one to be held in memory—slow and warm. Star reached up, hands on his cheeks, kissing his lips softly.

"I'll miss you, Ty. Will you send me a message ... when you have time? I'd love to hear about the characters dancing through your head."

"Only if you promise to do the same ... little baker girl. It's been quite a summer ... and now we're ... promise you'll tell me if you get any more anonymous envelopes." Ty chuckled. "And, I'll be back for one of your meatball mini-tarts with spicy cranberry sauce."

"Ty, I'm going to miss you. I mean ... really miss you."

He splayed his fingers over her cheeks, looked into her eyes, brushed his lips across hers, drew her tight.

Standing, not wanting to let go, wanting to remember the moment, etching it into their being, they finally let their arms drop.

Star dug her toe in the sand. Her heart beating so fast she could hardly breathe. Her eyes on the sand. "Ty, will you come home ... come home for the holidays?"

"Do you want me to?"

"More than I can say. Will you?"

Tyler gently lifted her chin so her eyes were looking into his.

Yes. I'll be back for the holidays."

"Promise?"

"Oh, yeah. I promise!"

The End

REVIEW REQUEST

If you enjoyed *One Summer*, please consider leaving an honest review on Amazon, even if it is only a line or two. It would mean a lot to me—what did you like best about the book, the characters?

Go to Amazon. Log in. Search: Mary Jane Forbes Baker Girl Series. Click the desired book. Click *Customer reviews* and then the *Write customer* review button.

Thank you!

ADD ME TO YOUR MAILING LIST

Please shoot me an email to be added to my mailing list for future book launches: MaryJane@MaryJaneForbes.com

Website: www.maryjaneforbes.com/

Acknowledgements

Three girl friends took up the challenge to come up with a story line for a diner waitress. They came through with flying colors. Thank you: Marcia Campbell, Peggy Keeney, Jeanne O'Brien, herein known as The Diner Sleuths.

Peggy Keeney – thanks again for hanging in there with me. Your keen eye and astute perspective are invaluable.

Geri Rogers—thanks for the research at the diner, the Butterworth Sisters, the author photo, manuscript review ... and, as always, your support.

Molly Tredwell—thank you, my supporter in chief, always looking at the big picture.

Roger and Pat Grady—thanks for your help and honest assessment. I appreciate your time spent on my projects.

Lois Gerber – thank you for accompanying me on a research project—above and beyond the definition of writer buddy.

Journey Into America, The Challenge of Islam, Akbar Ahmed, 2010, The Brookings Institution Press, Washington, D.C.

Saffron Dreams, Shaila Abdullah, 2009, Modern History Press, USA

The American Baking Competition, Season 1, CBS, Reality television, 2013.

Cover design: by Angie: pro_ebookcovers

About the Author

With each novel Mary Jane Forbes embarks on a new journey, a journey with old friends, making new friends along the way. She also sets out with a goal to learn more about something currently in the news. One Summer was such a journey. After a few false starts, the three main characters emerged—it then became their journey and Mary Jane held on for the ride.

Mary Jane retired to Florida and penned her first novel, "Murder in the House of Beads," in 2006. While she has written three short stories for children, her novels fall under the genre of Cozy Romance Mysteries filled with suspense.

She says her writing has been, and continues to be, an incredible journey. In researching her books she's met many wonderful people who shared insights on the tools of their trade and their experiences which were intriguing, inspiring and very educational.

A case in point, she met two new friends in writing "Twister—Ten Days in August." Because of the horrible tornados that swept from the Midwest to the East Coast in 2011 and 2012, she met the manufacturer of Twister-Safe Rooms. In the same novel, a sweet story of a Korean immigrant and his son Richard were brought to life inspired by a conversation with a new friend at a dinner party.

Writing the Murder by Design series, Mary Jane took a trip down memory lane to her parent's retirement home in Hansville, a village she and her sister visited many times traveling by ferry across Puget Sound from Seattle, Washington.

READ NEXT!

Promises, Star's Bakery

A mysterious donation. A deadly poisoning. One pastry chef must follow the cupcake crumbs to solve a murder… and save her bakery.

After a heartbreaking TV bake-off, Star Bloom thought her restaurant dreams were spoiled until an anonymous donor leaves her a small fortune. With her bakery's finishing touches nearly in place, she can't wait for the grand opening and an appearance from the special guest who stole her heart.

Tyler Jackman is living every animator's dream. But not even a big-budget movie contract can make him forget the beautiful girl he left behind. When his friend invites him back to town, he plans a romantic surprise that's sure to sweep her off her feet. But their celebration ends in a bitter aftertaste when Star's signature frosting shows up in a poisoned man's post-mortem.

With murder and thousands of miles between them, can Star and Tyler uncover the real killer—and their true feelings—before it's too late?

Promises is the second novel in The Baker Girl series of delicious romantic cozy mysteries. If you like scrumptious love stories, shocking twists, and a dash of hilarity, then you'll love Mary Jane Forbes' flavorful whodunit.

Buy *Promises* to sift out clues in a sweet romantic mystery today!

CPSIA information can be obtained
at www.ICGtesting.com
Printed in the USA
LVHW080828270620
659113LV00019B/464